Willie & Me

Sometimes you can change history.
And sometimes history can change you.

Willie & Me

A Baseball Card Adventure

Dan Gutman

HARPER

An Imprint of HarperCollinsPublishers

Library of Congress Cataloging-in-Publication Data
Gutman, Dan.
  Willie & me : a baseball card adventure / Dan Gutman.—First edition.
    pages cm
  Summary: "Joe 'Stosh' Stoshack uses his power to time travel using
baseball cards to go back to 1951, when Bobby Thomson hit the famous Shot
Heard Round the World home run to win the National League pennant for
the New York Giants"— Provided by publisher.
  ISBN 978-0-06-170404-8 (hardback)
  1. Polo Grounds (New York, N.Y.)—Fiction. [1. Time travel—Fiction.
2. Baseball—Fiction. 3. New York Giants (Baseball team)—Fiction.] I. Title.
II. Title: Willie and me.
PZ7.G9846Wi 2015   2014028436
[Fic]—dc23   CIP
                                                                             AC

Typography by Cara Petrus
17 18 19   CG/RRDH   10 9 8 7 6 5 4 3 2
❖
First Edition

To Ray and Eric Dimetrosky

Acknowledgments

THANKS TO MY EDITORS OF THIS SERIES SINCE 1996—Andrew Harwell, Barbara Lalicki, Rachel Orr, Elise Howard, Stephen Fraser, and Stephanie Siegel. Also my deepest gratitude to Liza Voges, Nina Wallace, Howard Wolf, Craig Proturny, David Kelly, Eric Levin, Robert Lifson, Joanne Pure, Pat Kelly and the good folks at the National Baseball Hall of Fame, SABR, Zach Rice, Steve Chorney for the fantastic covers, and Joshua Prager. And, of course, all the folks at HarperCollins.

Now it is done, now the story ends. And there is no way to tell it. The art of fiction is dead. Reality has strangled invention. Only the utterly impossible, the inexpressibly fantastic, can ever be plausible again.

—Red Smith,
New York Herald Tribune,
October 3, 1951

Introduction

WITH A BASEBALL CARD IN MY HAND, I AM THE MOST POW-
erful person in the world. With a card in my hand, I
can do something the president of the United States
can't do, the most intelligent genius on the planet
can't do, the best athlete in the universe can't do.

I can travel through time.

—Joe Stoshack

Flip Flops

"YOU'RE THE MAN, STOSH!" MY TEAMMATE LEON GREENE shouted through cupped hands from second base. "Let's *do* this thing, and get outta here."

It was drizzling when I came to bat in the sixth inning at Dunn Field. I hate playing in the rain. You can't dig your feet into the dirt of the batter's box, and it's easy to slip in the mud when you break for first base. I wiped my hands on my pants. The bat was slippery.

But then, so was the ball. I looked up at the Ace Hardware pitcher. He was a lefty, like me. His name was Lenny Breakowitz, or something like that. He didn't look too thrilled about playing in the rain either. His first pitch had bounced ten feet in front of the plate. Ball one. He was blowing on his fingers, trying to dry them off.

Now he was ready, and so was I. The pitch looked

fat. I took a rip at it, but missed. Swung too early. One and one. *Take a deep breath.*

The rain seemed to be coming down harder. I wiped my eyes with my sleeve. *Why doesn't the lady ump call the game?* It's not like it's the World Series or anything. The game doesn't *mean* anything. Let's go home.

Breakowitz looked in for his sign, nodded, and went into his windup. The pitch looked outside to me, so I let it go. Fortunately, the ump agreed. Ball two.

"Drive me in, Stosh!" Leon hollered from second. "Come on!"

I had almost forgotten that Leon was there, because I was looking at my new cleats. They were soaked all the way through. My mom was going to go ballistic. She just bought the cleats for my birthday yesterday, and they were already messed up. I glanced up toward the parents' section of the bleachers. It was empty. She must be waiting for me in the comfort of her car, like all the other parents who had any sense.

Focus, Stosh, I told myself. Two outs. Runner on second. Last inning. We were down by one run. A single could tie it.

I stepped out of the batter's box to wipe my hands and glance over at our coach, Flip Valentini, in the dugout. Flip's a really old guy who knows more about baseball than just about anybody. He's got arthritis and heart problems and a bum leg, but he's still out there every day coaching us. He just loves the game.

Honestly, I think it's what keeps him going. Flip could never retire.

I got ready for the next pitch. It was armpit level, but the ump called it a strike anyway. She probably wanted to go home as much as I did. I shouldn't be so choosy. Two and two.

"Okey-dokey!" Flip hollered at me, clapping his hands. "Fuhgetaboutit, Stosh!"

To the other team, that might have sounded like meaningless baseball chatter, but "Okey-dokey, fuh-getaboutit" is Flip's signal for a hit-and-run play. Now Leon's job was to run on the next pitch, and my job was to try and poke the ball through the infield.

Flip loves signs and signals. He's constantly inventing new ones for us to memorize. He also loves stealing signs from our opponents. Nothing makes him happier than when he can let us know what the other team is about to do, and then we stop them from doing it. I think it makes him feel more like he's part of the game.

One time I asked Flip if stealing signs was cheating, and he told me, "It ain't cheatin' if you don't get caught." According to Flip, cheating has been going on in baseball since the very beginning, when Abner Doubleday got credit for inventing the game even though he never played baseball in his life. But that's a story for another day.

Breakowitz took off his glasses and started wiping them on his sleeve.

"Just like I taught ya, Stosh," Flip said, clapping

his hands. "Go get 'im. It's all you, babe. All you."

Flip and I have a long history together, in more ways than one. Once, I took him back in time with me. No, *really*, I did. We got a Satchel Paige baseball card and went back to 1942 with a radar gun to see if Paige could throw a fastball a hundred miles an hour. We never did answer that question, but Satch taught Flip how to throw his famous hesitation pitch. He would swing his arm around like a windmill, and it seemed like the ball would leave his hand an instant after he released it. It must have been some kind of an optical illusion or something. But it threw off a batter's timing and was *really* hard to hit.

The other thing that happened while we were back in 1942 was that Flip fell for this cute waitress named Laverne. Her dad wasn't too happy about that, and he chased us around with a shotgun. Flip and I got separated, and I had to leave him in the past. It was pretty scary.

But there was a happy ending. When I got back to the present day, Flip and Laverne were married, and Flip was inducted into the Baseball Hall of Fame! It turned out that he lived his adult life all over again in the past, and the hesitation pitch made him a great pitcher. He won 287 games for the Brooklyn Dodgers, Cincinnati Reds, and Pittsburgh Pirates. It just goes to show.

But that's another story for another day, too. In the meantime, Breakowitz finished wiping off his glasses, and he was staring in for the sign.

My brain was on overload trying to remember all of the advice Flip had given me over the years. *Head up. Elbows in. Bend your knees. Relax. Focus. Guard the plate. Don't try to kill the ball. Just make contact.* And of course, that old chestnut: *Keep your eye on the ball.*

Duh. Where *else* would I possibly keep my eye?

"Just meet the ball, Stosh!" Flip shouted.

TMI. Too much information. My head felt like it was about to explode.

The rain was coming down harder. At this point, I didn't care if I got a hit or not. I just didn't want to look bad. Anything is better than a strikeout.

I pumped my bat twice. Breakowitz went into his windup. Leon took off from second. The pitch looked hittable. So I swung.

It wasn't any great wallop, I'll tell you that much. I made contact, a little bit up the barrel of my bat, too close to the handle. The vibration stung my hands. But I didn't care about that. I was digging for first.

I know we're supposed to watch the first-base coach and not look at the ball, but I couldn't resist. It was a little squib toward short, bouncing crazily. The shortstop had to scramble to his right to try and field the ball. It skittered past his outstretched glove, barely making it through the infield. I would be safe at first for sure and Leon was probably going to score and tie up the game. And if I could make it to second, I'd be in position to score the winning run. It would be a gamble, but maybe a gamble worth taking. I'm fairly fast, and our first-base coach, Leon's dad, was waving me around.

"Go! Go! Go!" everybody was screaming.

I knew the base path was muddy, so I was really careful not to slip and fall making the turn around first. I jammed my right foot against the left side of the bag to get an extra little boost toward second.

The left fielder was charging in to pick up the bouncing ball. I knew he had a choice. He could throw it home to try and get Leon, or throw it to second to get me. That option made more sense, and we both knew it.

"Slide, Stosh!" somebody yelled.

I love sliding. Sometimes I slide into a base even though I don't have to just because sliding is fun, and it looks cool, too. But I *had* to slide this time. I hit the dirt two strides in front of the bag and let my momentum carry me the rest of the way. The second baseman was crouched over the base, waiting for the throw.

One problem I hadn't thought of—you slide farther on a wet field. I felt myself moving too fast in the mud, past the bag. I tried to hook my foot on it, but it was too late. Then I tried reaching back with my hand to grab the base, but the second baseman's foot was blocking my way. He caught the ball cleanly and slapped the tag on my arm.

"Safe!" shouted the ump, who had run over to make the call. "I mean . . . out!"

That was it. The game was over.

It was my fault. I knew I was out fair and square, so I wasn't going to argue the call. I brushed some of the mud off my pants and jogged back to the dugout with my head down. But Flip's eyesight isn't that good anymore, and he just about freaked out in the dugout.

"Are you out of your *mind*?" he screamed at the ump. "He was *in* there!"

Flip jumped off the bench like a wild man and charged up the three steps to get to field level. He moves pretty well for an old guy with a busted leg from a spill he took back in his playing days. But like I said, his vision isn't so great and he must have misjudged the last step. Or maybe he just slipped.

I was crossing the third-base line when I saw it happen, almost in slow motion. I ran forward to try and grab him, but it was too late. The next thing anybody knew, Flip had fallen backward and landed hard on the concrete floor of the dugout. It all happened so fast that nobody had the chance to catch him. I just hoped he hadn't hit his head.

Everybody came rushing over, from our team and the other team too. Nobody cared about the final score or the outcome of the game anymore. Flip was hurt. He was on his back on the floor of the dugout.

"You okay, Mr. V?" asked the ump.

"I'm fine," Flip grunted, but it was obvious that he wasn't fine. "My man was safe at second and you know it. You just wanted to get the game over with so you could get out of the rain."

"Don't move, Mr. V," the ump told him, reaching for her cell phone. "We're going to get you a doctor."

"No doctors!" Flip shouted. "The last time I went to one of those quacks, it cost me four thousand bucks and Medicare wouldn't cover it."

"Can you get up?" one of the dads asked.

"I'll be okay," Flip grumbled. "Just gimme a minute."

He lay there for a bit, and then he tried to roll over on his side. But he couldn't do it. He groaned. You could see the pain on his face. He wasn't going anywhere.

Somebody must have called 911 because a couple of minutes later, an ambulance pulled up in the parking lot, its siren blaring. The paramedics got out, wheeling a stretcher.

2

Happy Birthday

I WANTED TO VISIT FLIP IN THE HOSPITAL THE NEXT DAY, which was Sunday. I figured I'd ride my bike over after church. But my mom told me Flip had had surgery in the middle of the night and would probably be drugged up on painkillers, so I should wait a day or two. She's a nurse at a hospital herself, so she knows about stuff like that.

It didn't matter anyway, because I spend Sunday afternoon with my dad. He moved into an apartment on the other side of town after he and my mom split up a few years ago. We get together most weeks. My mom sort of hides upstairs when Dad comes to pick me up, so she won't have to make chitchat with him.

"Where are we going?" I asked when Dad pulled up in his van.

"It's a surprise," was all he would tell me.

My dad's van is custom-made so it can be driven

without foot pedals. In fact, it doesn't even *have* foot pedals. The brake and the accelerator are levers on the right side of the steering wheel. They make vans like that for handicapped people. My dad was in a car accident a while back that left him paralyzed from the waist down. That's another story for another day. Anyway, he gets around pretty well for a guy whose legs are useless. But I help him, too. His wheelchair is in the back of the van.

We pulled up to the Louisville Marriott Hotel on West Jefferson Street, parked the van, and went inside. Dad still wouldn't tell me what was going on, but then I saw a sign in the lobby that said BASEBALL MEMORABILIA SHOW TODAY.

I've been collecting cards since I was little, and my dad is the one who got me started. He's been collecting since he was a kid, so he's got a lot of good stuff from the sixties, seventies, and eighties—Nolan Ryan, Hank Aaron, Tom Seaver, you know. That era. I don't usually go in for card shows myself. I'd rather add to my collection the old-fashioned way—you buy a pack of cards, peel off the wrapper, and then you get to see what goodies are inside. Is there any other product people buy where you don't know what you're buying? I can't think of one. It's just more exciting and mysterious to buy packs of cards than it is to buy cards that some dealer has on display. Cheaper, too. That's just my opinion.

My dad has been talking a lot lately about starting a little business buying and selling sports memorabilia online, so I guess he wanted to check out the show.

"Maybe you can help me," he said as we got on the elevator. "Hey, if this works out, you could be my partner and take over the business someday."

I'm not really interested in becoming a memorabilia dealer, but I didn't tell him because I didn't want to hurt his feelings. He hasn't had a lot of luck with jobs. Maybe this could be the break he needs.

The show was in a big ballroom at the hotel, with hundreds of tables lined up and dealers from all over the country. They were selling lots of stuff—bobblehead dolls, signed bats, balls, photos, game-worn jerseys, but mostly cards. There must have been a million baseball cards in that room. If the hotel were to catch on fire, well, a lot of people's life savings would be wiped out pretty quickly.

We went up and down the aisles looking at stuff, and Dad stopped to chat with a few of the dealers, but he didn't buy anything. I don't think he was looking for anything in particular. He was just trying to get the lay of the land and see how much people were charging.

Then he rolled his wheelchair to a table with a big sign over it that said BLASTS FROM THE PAST. A guy with a scraggly beard and a Dodgers T-shirt was standing behind the table. He stuck out his hand and introduced himself as Kenny.

"What can I do you for?" Kenny asked.

"I want to get a present for my son's birthday,"

Dad said. "He just turned fourteen two days ago."

"You don't have to buy me anything, Dad," I told him.

I know my father doesn't have a lot of money. He has a tough enough time paying his rent without worrying about buying me stuff that I don't need.

Kenny told us he specializes in home runs—baseballs that were hit for home runs, photos of players hitting homers, stuff like that. He showed us what he had, but it was all either really expensive or not all that interesting. We were about to move on to the next booth, but Kenny saw he was losing a possible customer and he reached under the table. He rooted around in a box down there for a moment.

"Maybe you'd be interested in *this*," he said. "I just got it in yesterday."

He pulled out a rectangular wooden plaque with two baseball cards mounted on it, one on either side. It was dusty. The cards looked like this. . . .

 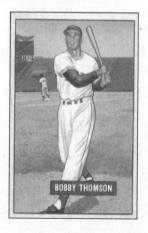

Between them, inscribed on a gold plate, were the words THE SHOT HEARD ROUND THE WORLD.

Ralph Branca and Bobby Thomson. I had heard of those guys. There was a documentary on TV about them. I saw it years ago. One of them was the batter and the other was the pitcher. I didn't remember the details.

"It was the most famous home run in baseball history," my dad said. "Nineteen fifty-two, am I right?"

"Fifty-one," Kenny said, wiping off the plaque with his sleeve. "Before my time."

"Mine too," said my dad. "The Dodgers against the Giants, right? That was the *New York* Giants. It was before both teams moved to California, Joey."

"I *know*, Dad," I said, rolling my eyes.

I'm not stupid. I know my baseball history. In 1958, the New York Giants became the San Francisco Giants, and the Brooklyn Dodgers became the Los Angeles Dodgers.

"The Giants won the first game of the 1951 season," Kenny told us, "and then they lost eleven in a row. They were terrible. By August eleventh, they were thirteen and a half games behind the Dodgers. It was hopeless."

"Then they turned it around," Dad said, picking up the story. "They won something like sixteen in a row."

"Thirty-seven of their last forty-four," Kenny said. "Twelve of their last thirteen. And on the last day of the season, they tied the Dodgers and forced a three-game playoff for the pennant."

"And in the final game . . . the final inning," Dad said, "Thomson hit the Shot Heard Round the World. Branca threw the pitch, that poor bum."

"The Giants win the pennant! The Giants win the pennant! The Giants win the pennant!" both of them started chanting.

I had heard that famous radio call of the home run myself. And I'd seen the video on YouTube.

"How much do you want for the plaque?" my dad asked.

Kenny looked it over, even pulling out a magnifying glass to examine both cards carefully.

"I can let it go for a hundred and fifty," he said.

My dad whistled.

"That's *way* too much," I whispered in his ear. "I don't want you to spend—"

"It's your birthday," he whispered back. "You only turn fourteen once. And besides, it's a *steal*. Thomson and Branca cards from 1951 have *got* to be worth more than a hundred and fifty bucks."

Dad turned back to Kenny.

"Mind if I ask why you're selling this so cheap?"

"The cards would be worth about a hundred each in mint condition," Kenny told us. "But they're creased and messed up a little at the edges. Also, they're glued to the wood. The guy who did that was a real dope. That always hurts the value. Too bad he didn't use photo corners. So anyway, they're not worth much."

"We'll think it over," my dad said, preparing to roll away.

"Tell you what," Kenny said before we could get very far. "You seem like good guys, and it's the kid's birthday. For you, I'll knock off ten percent. Make it a hundred and thirty-five. I shouldn't be doing this, but you caught me in a good mood."

My dad didn't think it over very long.

"We'll take it," he said.

"Dad! That's too much money!"

"Hey," Kenny said, "tell you what I'm gonna do. I'll give the plaque to ya for *free* if you can answer this question. Ya ready? When Thomson hit the Shot Heard Round the World, who was the on-deck batter? I'll give you one guess."

My dad looked at me blankly. He didn't know. I tried to think back and remember that documentary I saw on TV. But for the life of me, I couldn't come up with the name.

"I give up," I finally said.

"Willie Mays!" said Kenny. "Mays was in the on-deck circle when Thomson hit that homer."

"Yes!" I shouted, hitting my forehead. "I *knew* that!"

"Well, *here's* something you probably don't know," Kenny said as he handed me the plaque. "The Giants cheated. There's no way a team could come back from thirteen games behind that late in the season. They won the pennant by cheating."

"Ah, that's just sour grapes," my dad said as he

fished out his wallet and pulled out a bunch of bills. "You're a Dodger fan. It's been more than sixty years. Get over it."

"It's true, man," Kenny said. "They cheated. They won the pennant that year under false pretenses."

He was still calling the Giants cheaters as I rolled Dad away. I put the plaque in the big pocket in the back of his wheelchair. I tried to think of a place I could hang it on my wall, alongside some of the other baseball memorabilia I had been accumulating.

We looked at a few more booths at the show, but my dad seemed like he was dragging, so I suggested we hit the road. He gets tired easily.

"How much did that Kenny guy say the Thomson and Branca cards would be worth if they were autographed?" Dad asked me in the car as he drove me home.

"He didn't say."

"I bet it would be a lot," Dad told me. "A couple of thousand, at least. If only there was a way. . . ."

His voice trailed off. I looked at him. He was watching the road. But I knew what he was thinking.

"No!" I told him. "I am *not* going to go back to 1951 just to get Bobby Thomson and Ralph Branca to sign their baseball cards."

"I didn't say a word!" Dad protested.

"But you were thinking it!"

"Well, yeah, I *was* thinking it," Dad admitted. "It would be an easy score. You just go back, get the autographs, and split. Boom. Done. A thousand bucks easy."

But it *wouldn't* be easy. I knew that from experience. It was never easy. Something always happened.

"I won't do it, Dad," I said. And that was the end of it.

This is what my dad always does. He comes up with these get-rich-quick schemes that involve me traveling back in time so he can make money. One time, he scraped together five thousand dollars so I could deposit it in a bank in 1932, and he could make a fortune on the interest.

There's probably nothing illegal about that, but it just doesn't seem *right*. It feels dishonest. In my mind, if I'm going to use my power to go back in time, I'm going to do it for a good reason. Maybe help somebody who needs it or right some wrong. I wouldn't do it just to make money.

On the other hand, he *is* my dad. And I know he has money problems. It would be pretty cool to buy something for a hundred and thirty-five dollars and then turn around and sell it for thousands.

We drove in silence for a few minutes, but I could tell he was still thinking about how much money we could make if the Thomson and Branca cards were signed.

"That's how rich people get richer, you know," he told me as he pulled up to the house. "They figure out an advantage, and then they use their advantage. That's what separates the really successful people from the rest of us bums. You think Bill Gates never bent the rules a little to get ahead? Or Donald

Trump? Or that guy who started Facebook, what's his name?"

"Mark Zuckerberg," I said.

"Yeah, that guy. Look, the plaque is yours to keep. It's your birthday present, Joe. You can do what you want with it. But think about it. That's all I ask."

"Okay," I said. "I'll think about it."

3

One Lousy Pitch

My birthday party was that night. Well, it wasn't really a "party." I haven't had a birthday party since I was nine years old. But my mom and my uncle Wilbur, who lives with us, invited a few guys on my team over for pizza and cake.

After I blew out the candles, Mom totally surprised me with a present that my grandmother had sent me—a little video camera. The thing isn't much bigger than a cell phone, but it has a lens that lets you zoom in on objects that are really far away and fill the whole screen with them. Very cool. I had never really been into movies or photography, but I thought it might be fun to shoot some videos and put them up on YouTube or something.

Eventually, everybody went home, leaving me alone in the living room eating birthday cake with my uncle Wilbur, who is very old and sick. Actually, he wouldn't be alive at *all* if not for me. It's true. What happened was that when Uncle Wilbur was a boy back in 1919, he caught influenza and was probably going to die. *Millions* of people died in that epidemic. As it turned out, I was traveling back to 1919 to see Shoeless Joe Jackson of the Chicago White Sox. I was taking flu medicine myself at the time, and I had it with me when I bumped into my great uncle at the ballpark. They didn't have any medicine to treat the flu back then. So I gave him mine, and when I got back to the present day, Uncle Wilbur was alive. He recovered because of the flu medicine I gave him.

But that's a story for another day, too.

Uncle Wilbur is not a huge baseball fan like me, but I showed him the plaque my dad had given me as a birthday present.

"Did you ever hear of Bobby Thomson?" I asked.

"Sure," he replied. "He hit the Shot Heard Round the World. It was 1951. Dodgers and Giants. I remember. *Everybody* who was alive back then remembers. But it wasn't Thomson who I remember so much. It was the other guy, Ralph Branca."

"What about him?"

"That one lousy pitch ruined Branca's life," he told me. "The guy had a decent career. He was a good pitcher. Big guy. But for the rest of his life, the only thing anybody knew about him was that he threw that one lousy pitch. He lost the pennant for the Dodgers. He was the all-time biggest goat in baseball history. Ya couldn't help but feel sorry for the guy. Everybody did."

After we cleaned up the paper plates and stuff, I went upstairs. I wasn't tired yet, so I started leafing through a few of my old baseball books. That guy Kenny at the card show pretty much had his facts right. The Giants had been having a terrible season, and then they turned it around in the last few weeks and caught the Dodgers on the last day. They won the pennant when Bobby Thomson hit the homer off Ralph Branca in the final game of the three-game playoff. It happened at the Polo Grounds in New York, a ballpark I knew well.

I looked up Bobby Thomson and Ralph Branca in *The Baseball Encyclopedia*, this thick reference book that has the statistics on every player who ever made a major league appearance. Neither of them were superstars. Thomson had a lifetime batting average of .270, and he only reached .300 one year. He never hit more than thirty-two homers in a season. He was good, but not great. Branca had an 88–68 lifetime record, and he topped twenty wins in just one season. Neither of those guys had Hall of Fame numbers. But because of that one lousy pitch in 1951, they were famous.

I opened up my laptop and did a Google search for both of them. All I had to type was "Ralph B" and Branca came up as the third listing. There were two and a half *million* results. It wasn't so easy with Bobby Thomson because there are lots of Thomsons out there, some of them spelled with a P in the middle.

I went to Google Images and searched for "Ralph Branca." There were lots of photos of him. He was a handsome guy, with jet-black hair, bushy dark eyebrows, and a big nose. One of the pictures grabbed my attention, and it was repeated over and over again. It was a photo of Branca taken minutes after he gave up the Shot Heard Round the World.

He still has his uniform on and he's sitting on the steps of the Dodger clubhouse with his elbows on his knees and his hands together, almost like he's praying. His head is bent way down. You can't see his face, but you don't have to. The guy was obviously crushed. He had just experienced the worst moment of his life. He was only twenty-five years old. But he probably knew right then that he would be remembered for throwing that one lousy pitch—and nothing else—forever.

It was the worst moment in Ralph Branca's life.

I picked up the plaque that my dad had given me and looked at the two cards through a magnifying glass. I wondered what it must have been like for Thomson and Branca—two regular guys who became famous for what happened in one split second of their lives. One swing of the bat. Thomson became a hero and Branca became a loser. If it hadn't been for that one swing of the bat, they both would have just faded into obscurity like the thousands of other regular guys who played over the years. I guess you never know when a moment in your lifetime might come that will totally change everything.

I must have been sleepier than I thought. At some point I lay back on my bed and closed my eyes. Still holding the plaque and thinking about the Shot Heard Round the World, I dozed off.

Sometime in the middle of the night, I heard a noise. I never heard the window open or the floor creaking. But even in my sleep, I instinctively knew that someone had broken into my room. I bolted upright in my bed and saw the vague outline of a figure in the shadows about ten feet away. It was too dark to make out any of his features. The only light was from my little night-light by the door.

"What the—"

I grabbed for the first solid object I could find—the wooden plaque that my father had given me for my birthday. I jumped out of bed and swung the plaque as hard as I could at the guy in my room. I tried to smash it into his face.

"Oww!" the guy said. "Stop it! What are you, crazy?"

The guy was bigger than me—maybe six three and two hundred pounds. He grabbed the plaque and ripped it out of my hands. I was defenseless.

"Don't hurt me!" I begged. "Take my money! Take whatever you want!"

"I don't want your money!" the guy said, handing the plaque back to me. "I just want to talk. Man, you've got a good swing there!"

My eyes were starting to adjust to the light. Now I could see he was wearing a baseball uniform. It said "Brooklyn" across the front in that old-fashioned style of lettering. He had a Saint Christopher medal around his neck.

"Joey, is everything okay?" my mom called from downstairs. "What's that noise?"

"Shhhhh!" I said to the guy in the Dodger uniform. Then I called downstairs, "I just had a dream, Mom. I fell out of bed."

"Are you okay? Do you need me to come upstairs?" she hollered.

"No! It's all good."

I realized my heart was beating really fast. The guy in the Dodger uniform was standing in front of me, his hands in the air as if I were pointing a gun at him. He didn't look threatening.

"Who *are* you?" I asked him, lowering my voice.

"Is your name Joe Stoshack?" the guy whispered. "They call you Stosh?"

"Yeah."

He brought his hands down and stuck one out to shake. "I'm Ralph Branca," he said.

Ralph Branca

I sat back on my bed.

"You gotta be kidding me! The real Ralph Branca?" I asked. "The guy who gave up the home run to Bobby Thomson?"

Branca sighed and rolled his eyes, like he was sick of hearing that. He *did* look like the guy I had seen in the photos. Dark hair. Bushy eyebrows. Big nose. But I couldn't be positive.

"Nobody remembers that I won twenty-one games

when I was just twenty-one years old," he told me. "Nobody remembers that I had seventy-five wins when I was just twenty-five. All they remember is that I threw that stinking pitch to Thomson. Ah, forget it."

"Am I dreaming?" I asked.

"I don't know," he replied. "Maybe *I* am."

"I just dozed off, and when I woke up you were here," I told him.

"And I was just warming up in the bullpen, and the next thing I knew I was here," he replied.

I remembered that something like this happened once before. A long time ago. It was my first experience with time travel. I went to sleep and in the middle of the night I woke up to find the great Honus Wagner sitting in my bedroom. That *really* freaked me out.

"Do you know what year it is?" I asked Branca.

"Of course," he replied. "It's 1953. Why?"

I went over to my desk, picked up my calendar, and handed it to him. He sat on my bed with a thud.

"That means it works," he said softly.

"*What* works?" I asked. "Hey, how did you know my name? Is this some kind of a scam?"

"A friend of mine told me about a kid named Joe Stoshack who could travel through time and take people with him," Branca said. "With baseball cards."

A friend of his? What friend? Only a few people in the whole world knew about my special power. My parents. Flip Valentini. My cousin Samantha, who of course had to go and tell her best friend, Chelsea McCormack. Bobby Fuller . . .

"What friend?" I asked.

"A guy on my team."

"What guy?"

"Jackie Robinson," he said.

Of course! For a school project, I had traveled back to 1947 and met Jackie Robinson. I was there the day he broke the color barrier. Jackie played on the Dodgers, too. He must have told Branca about me. And I had a feeling that I knew why Branca wanted to talk to me.

"You might have heard this, but a couple of years ago," he said, "we had this game against the Giants. It was a big game, a *really* big game. We had a two-run lead. And they brought me in to close it out in the ninth inning. And I—"

"I know all about it," I told him. I didn't want him to have to tell the painful story one more time.

"So I was wondering . . . if maybe you could . . . y'know . . ."

"Make it not happen?" I guessed.

"Yeah," Branca replied, lowering his head. "Make it not happen. Do something so it didn't happen. Make it go away."

"I don't know if I can do that," I told him honestly.

It wasn't just that I was reluctant to help the guy out. I had tried to go back in time and change history before. I tried to prevent the Black Sox Scandal from happening and save Shoeless Joe Jackson's reputation. I tried to warn President Roosevelt that Pearl Harbor was going to be attacked. I tried to prevent Ray Chapman and Roberto Clemente from getting killed tragically. Each time, I had failed. Maybe history just doesn't *want* to be changed. History wants to be left alone.

"I just thought that maybe you could go back and . . . I don't know, change things," Branca said softly. "I'm tired of being introduced as the guy who gave up that home run. I can't walk down my own street without somebody reminding me about that pitch. At home at night, I have nightmares about it. That one pitch ruined my life. No matter what I do until the day I die, that's all anyone's going to remember about me."

He looked so sad, almost desperate.

"If you rob a bank, they throw you in jail, and at some point you get paroled," Branca told me. "Sometimes even murderers get out of jail. But I'll *never* be forgiven for what I did. Do you understand what I'm saying? I want another chance. Can you help me?"

I thought it over.

"Will you sign this baseball card for me?" I asked, handing him the plaque.

"Sure, kid, anything."

I got a pen from my desk drawer, and Branca signed the card.

"I'll see what I can do," I told him. I wasn't sure I would be able to help Branca out, but I didn't want the poor guy to have a miserable life forever, either.

"Thanks, Stosh," he said, shaking my hand again. "So, how do I get out of here?"

"Probably the same way you got here in the first place."

I climbed back into bed with the plaque in my arms, closed my eyes, and tried to will myself back to sleep. It was probably just a dream, I remember thinking. It *had* to be a dream. Baseball players don't just show up in your bedroom in the middle of the night.

When I opened my eyes the next morning, Ralph Branca was gone. The first thing I did was look at the plaque.

His baseball card was signed.

It really happened.

4

"I Ain't Dead Yet"

My hometown, Louisville, Kentucky, is on the Ohio River, about halfway between Indianapolis and Nashville. It's a pretty cool city, I think. Churchill Downs is here. That's where the Kentucky Derby is run every year. The Muhammad Ali Center is out on Museum Row, and Colonel Harlan Sanders, the guy who started KFC, is buried in Cave Hill Cemetery. For baseball fans like me, there's the Louisville Slugger Museum. They have a huge bat outside. It's 120 feet tall and 68,000 pounds. I've been there a few times.

The next day after school, my mom drove me over to Norton Audubon Hospital. It's just a few miles from our house, across the street from Clark Park. The lady at the front desk told us that Flip was in the ICU, which stands for Intensive Care Unit. It's on the third floor.

The Louisville Slugger Museum

Hospitals are creepy. There were a lot of old people in the rooms we walked by, and some of them were lying on rolling beds in the hallways. Some of them were in bad shape. We had trouble finding Flip's room, so we had to ask a nurse. She told us where to go and added, "You can't miss it."

She was right. We couldn't miss it. There were so many flowers and balloons, they were spilling out of the room and into the hallway.

Flip acts like such a regular guy that sometimes I forget how famous he is. But as soon as Flip got hurt, the story hit the newspapers and the Internet, and get-well wishes must have poured in from people all over the country.

When we opened the door, Flip was sleeping. His wife, Laverne, was sitting next to the bed looking out the window. She smiled and got up to greet us, giving me a big hug as she always does. Laverne knows that she and Flip never would have met if it hadn't been for me taking him back to 1942.

She brought us over to the far corner of the room so we could talk without waking up Flip.

"How's he doing?" my mom whispered.

"It was a femoral neck fracture," Laverne whispered back. "It's bad, but the doctor told me the operation went well."

I figured that meant Flip broke his neck, but my mom is a nurse and she told me a femoral neck fracture is in the hip. As we get older, apparently, our bones get thinner and weaker. It's much easier for a guy Flip's age to break a hip. It's also really serious with older people because a hip fracture can trigger other problems and dangerous complications after surgery, like blood clots, infection, and pneumonia. Mom and Laverne talked about a bunch of other medical stuff, but most of it went over my head.

"Could Flip die?" I asked.

"Possibly," Laverne replied. "The doctor told me that mortality rates in the year following a hip fracture are very high for men of Flip's age."

"That ain't gonna happen," said a rough voice from the other side of the room. "Fuhgetaboutit. I ain't dead yet."

"Flip!" I said, rushing over to his bedside. I

grabbed his hand. Flip's voice was weak, but he had a smile on his face and a strong grip. "How are you feeling?"

"I won't be dancin' anytime soon," he replied. "That'll teach me not to argue with umpires, huh, Stosh?"

My mom came over, gave him a kiss on the cheek, and asked if there was anything she could do for him while he was laid up in the hospital.

"Yeah," he replied. "Have your kid go back in time a couple of days and stop me from fallin' on my butt."

"Language, dear!" Laverne scolded him. "There are children present."

"What, ya think Stosh never heard that word before?" Flip asked. "I'm an old fart and I could drop dead any minute. So I'm allowed to say what I want."

Flip was in good spirits. Laverne told us she was sure he would make a full recovery, but it might take a year for him to walk again. Flip joked that he didn't mind, because Laverne would have to push him around in a wheelchair all the time.

"Why don't we leave these two boys alone for a while so they can talk boy talk?" Laverne said, escorting my mom into the hallway.

I pulled a chair up close to Flip's bed so I could hear him better.

"Listen, Stosh," he said hoarsely, "I need to talk to you about somethin'. I'm not gonna be able to coach the team next season. They're gonna have to get somebody else."

"I know," I assured him. "Don't worry about that."

"Another thing. Laverne and I decided that when I finally get out of this joint, I should retire for good. Close down the store, liquidate the inventory. You know, the whole nine yards."

"You're going to turn all those baseball cards into a liquid?" I asked. "Why? How would you even do that?"

"No, you dope!" Flip shouted, coughing. "Liquidate means to sell off all the stuff. I'm gonna get rid of it all. So if you want anything, you can have it before the vultures descend on the store and clean it out. I got a lot of good cards in there, you know, Stosh. You might want to use some of them to, uh . . . do that thing you do. The time travel thing."

Wow. That was some offer. Flip had *thousands* of baseball cards, from every decade. They could keep me busy for the rest of my life.

"Thanks, Flip," I told him, and then I lowered my voice. "You know, speaking of cards, I need to talk to you about something, too."

"Shoot, Stosh."

"Remember I told you about the night Honus Wagner showed up in my bedroom a few years ago?"

"Yeah. That was when you first found out about your . . . power."

"Right," I said. "Well, I had *another* visitor last night."

"Was it Cobb?" Flip asked, his eyes wide.

"No."

"Lou Gehrig? DiMaggio? Stan the Man Musial?" Flip guessed.

"No," I told him. "Ralph Branca."

"Ralphie?" Flip smiled as he struggled to sit up in the bed. "The guy who threw the pitch that Bobby Thomson hit over the wall to win the 1951 pennant for the Giants?"

"That's the guy," I replied. "Did you know him?"

"Sure I knew him," Flip told me. "He was my teammate. We were on the Dodgers together. But tell me this—how did you know the guy in your room was Ralph Branca? He coulda been anybody."

"He looked like the pictures I've seen of Branca," I said. "He was wearing a Dodger uniform and he knew stuff that only Ralph Branca would know. He was depressed because he had a good career going, but then he threw that one pitch to Thomson and it ruined his life."

"It made him famous, too," Flip told me. "Did he mention that? Nobody ever would know Ralphie's name today if he hadn't served up that gopher ball to Thomson."

"He doesn't see it that way," I told Flip. "He doesn't want to be famous for being a loser. He says he can't walk down the street without people pointing at him and whispering. Everybody he meets asks him how he feels about losing the pennant. He wants his life back, and he thinks I can give it to him. He wants me to erase the mistake."

Flip sighed and shook his head.

"We *all* wanna go back in time and erase the mistakes we made when we were young and stupid," he said. "How did Branca know you can travel through time with baseball cards, anyway?"

"Jackie Robinson told him."

"Of course," Flip said, nodding.

"So what do you think?" I asked. "Should I do it?"

Flip leaned back on his pillow and stared at the ceiling for a while. I gave him the time to think things over.

"Let me ask you this," he finally said. *"How* would you do it? What could you do to help him, anyway?"

"I'm not sure," I admitted. "There are a *million* things I could do to stop Thomson from hitting that homer. I could go back to 1951 and tell Branca to walk Thomson intentionally. That would make sense. First base was open. Or I could tell him to throw a different pitch. I could pull out an air horn and blast it at the moment Thomson is about to swing. I could poison Thomson's food before the game. Hey, I could poison *Branca's* food so he can't pitch that day. Something. *Anything.* It wouldn't take much."

Flip crossed his arms in front of him and closed his eyes. I thought that he might be taking a nap, but he was just thinking things over.

"Life is life," Flip finally said. "What happened, happened. Ninety-nine percent of the time I would say don't do it. Don't mess with history. You could make things worse. But . . ."

"But what?"

"But I see both sides," Flip continued. "Sometimes, breakin' the rules can be the right thing to do."

"What do you mean?" I asked.

"Who am I to say you shouldn't help Ralphie?" Flip told me. "If you hadn't taken me back with you and changed my past, I never woulda had a career in baseball. People wouldn'ta sent me all these flowers and cards and stuff. And most important, I never woulda met Laverne."

"You might not be in this hospital bed either," I pointed out.

"Hey, if it weren't for you, Stosh, I might not be in *any* bed," Flip said. "I might be in a casket. If you ask me, I say give Branca another chance to live his life over again, just like you did for me."

Flip closed his eyes again. I could tell he was tired.

At that point, I decided I would do it.

5

Another Visitor

THE NEXT STEP WOULD BE TO BREAK THE NEWS TO MY mother. Mom's a bit, you could say, *overprotective*. So I had to be careful how I handled things. I waited until she was in a good mood. It was after dinner the next day. I washed the dishes while she dried. She told me a funny story about something that happened at work that day, but I wasn't really paying attention.

"Mom," I said right out, "I want to go on another trip."

She stopped wiping the dish in her hands.

"You mean . . ."

"Yeah," I said. "*That* kind of trip."

I told her all about the Shot Heard Round the World and about my visit from Ralph Branca. I said the reason I wanted to go back to 1951 was to help him out.

As expected, Mom wasn't too crazy about the idea. She gave me all her usual objections: I might get lost in New York. I might get stuck in 1951. I might get hurt, and the medical care wasn't as good in the old days. On and on like that. She softened a bit when I told her that Flip said helping Branca was the right thing to do. I promised not to go on a school night, and she made me promise to take some food, Band-Aids, and an umbrella with me.

"Okay, okay," she finally agreed. "You can go. But be *careful*."

Well, that was a relief. I really wasn't sure she was going to give me her blessing, because every time I've gone on a trip so far, something has gone wrong. I've landed in the wrong place, or the wrong time. I've found myself in the middle of a war zone, with bullets flying around my head. I've been chased down the street by a maniac with a baseball bat. I've been kidnapped by gamblers, locked in a closet, and stuck inside a fighter plane that crash-landed.

Of course, I didn't tell my mother about *all* the bad stuff that has happened to me while traveling through time. If she knew, she would never let me go *anywhere*.

But this time, I decided, *nothing* was going to go wrong. This time, I was going to be ready for *anything*. Because I was going to do my research.

After school the next day, I rode my bike over to the Louisville Free Public Library on York Street. It's easy to look stuff up online, I know, and I do that a lot. But I also like to go into the stacks in the library and get lost in the books.

First, I wanted to find out what October 1951 would be like. The reference librarian showed me a book that listed important events that happened throughout history. The Korean War had started the year before, and it was raging. In July 1951, it was announced that the transistor had been invented, and it revolutionized electronics. You could go to a gas station and buy a gallon for nineteen cents, believe it or not. It was a different world.

The Catcher in the Rye came out that year. Patti Page was singing "Tennessee Waltz." *The King and I* was a hit on Broadway. In the movies, people were watching *A Streetcar Named Desire*, *The African Queen*, *An American in Paris*, and *Abbott and Costello Meet the Invisible Man*. Hardly anybody had a TV back then, but the people who did were watching *I Love Lucy*, *The Jack Benny Show*, *What's My Line*, and *Bozo the Clown*.

All that stuff was good to know, but more importantly, I needed to know exactly when, where, and how Bobby Thomson was going to hit that home run off Ralph Branca. It didn't take long to find all the details. There are entire books written about that game.

It took place on Wednesday, October 3, at the Polo Grounds in New York City. I had been there before. I met Jim Thorpe at the Polo Grounds in 1913 and Ray Chapman in 1920. I even remembered the cross streets—West 155th Street and Eighth Avenue. It was near a river, I recalled.

As I read about the end of the game, I tried to picture it in my head so I would be ready when I got there. It was the bottom of the ninth inning. The Brooklyn Dodgers were leading the New York Giants 4–1, and the Giants were getting their "last licks."

Don Newcombe was pitching for the Dodgers. Alvin Dark singled to right field to start things off. Then Don Mueller hit another single, sending Dark to third. Runners on first and third. Monte Irvin fouled out to first. One out.

The next batter, Whitey Lockman, hit a double to left, scoring Dark. The score was 4–2 now. When Mueller slid into third base safely, he twisted his ankle so badly that he had to be carried off-field. A pinch runner was brought in—Clint Hartung.

There were runners on second and third, with the tying run at second and the winning run at the plate. That's when Bobby Thomson came up. Willie Mays was on deck.

At that point, Don Newcombe was taken out of the game and Ralph Branca came in to relieve him. This was the big moment. Branca threw his first pitch right over the plate and Thomson looked at it. Strike one.

It was Branca's second pitch that turned into the Shot Heard Round the World. All accounts said the pitch was high and inside. Thomson had no business swinging at it. But somehow, he managed to get around on the ball and tomahawk it down the left field line. It landed in the lower deck that hung slightly over the field, and that was it.

One of the books in the library had a photograph that was taken the instant Thomson hit the ball. You could even see it in the air.

The Shot Heard Round the World

The Giants won the game 5–4, and the National League pennant, of course. New York went crazy. Two people at the Polo Grounds were so shocked that they suffered heart attacks.

So that's what I would be dealing with. That's the situation I would have to undo. Hit the reset button. I would have to come up with *some* way to change history, for Ralph Branca's sake.

The next day, my mom surprised me by giving me an envelope with thirty dollars in it—in 1951 money. She said she knew a guy who collected old money, and she thought I might need some. Uncle Wilbur, who is just about my size, gave me an old pair of his pants, shoes, and a shirt so I would fit in with what guys wore back in 1951. If I showed up wearing Nikes and a T-shirt that said just about *anything* on it, people would be suspicious. I was going to be prepared this time.

I decided to make my trip the following night, Friday. On Thursday, I sat up in bed reading Ralph Branca's autobiography, *A Moment in Time*, which I had checked out of the library. It was interesting to read about the relationship between Ralph and Bobby. For years after the Shot Heard Round the World, the two men barely spoke. Then later, they got to know each other and realized they could make money from the historic event they had shared. In fact, on the fiftieth anniversary of "the Shot," they each earned $220,000 by autographing bats, balls, photos, and jerseys.

Wow, that's a lot of money for signing your name.

I dozed off reading the book. I was as ready as I would ever be. Nothing could go wrong.

Until something did.

* * *

In the middle of the night, I heard a noise. Yes, *again.* Somebody was in my room. I figured it was Branca again. He was probably angry that I hadn't changed history yet.

"Ralph?" I whispered. "Mr. Branca?"

"No," said a man's voice.

I strained to see him. He wasn't wearing a Dodgers uniform. He was wearing a *Giants* uniform.

"Who are you?" I asked.

"My name is Bobby Thomson."

"You *gotta* be kidding me!"

I sat up in bed and flipped on the light at my bedside so I could see him better. He was a tall man with dark hair, and his eyes were wide apart.

Bobby Thomson

"Is your name Joe Stoshack?" Bobby finally asked. "The kid who can travel through time with baseball cards?"

"How do *you* know who I am?" I said. "How did you find out about me?"

"Word gets around, Joe," Bobby said. "People talk."

"What are you doing here?" I asked.

"I want to ask you a favor."

"What is it?"

He pulled my desk chair up to the side of my bed.

"I hit a home run back in 1951," he whispered. "You might have heard about it. It was a pretty big one."

"I know all about it," I replied. "They call it the Shot Heard Round the World."

"Yeah. I understand that Ralph Branca was here."

I nodded. I had a feeling about what he was going to say.

"And Branca asked you to go back in time and do something—I don't know what—to prevent me from hitting that homer."

"Um-hmm," I said.

"Well, I'm asking you *not* to do that," Bobby said.

That's exactly what I thought he was going to say. I didn't know how to respond.

"Look," Bobby continued. "I'm not a star. They'll never vote me into the Baseball Hall of Fame. Other than that one swing, that one home run, I'm just an ordinary player. But that homer was the greatest thing that ever happened to me. It made me famous. It put me on the map, and I got a feeling it's gonna help put my kids and grandkids through college. Please don't interfere with what happened naturally. Just let it be. What's done is done."

He looked sad, almost as sad as Ralph Branca had looked when he was in my room a few nights earlier.

"I . . . I don't know, Mr. Thomson," I told him.

Now I was confused. I had decided I was going to go back and help Branca the next night. But Thomson was asking me *not* to help Branca.

The expression on Bobby's face seemed more serious.

"Joe," he said, "everybody likes to win. I like to win. You don't get to the top in professional baseball, or any other business, unless you're a pretty tough cookie. My team likes to win, too, and that was a great victory for me and the guys. I play with some competitive people. If you do anything to mess things up for us . . ."

"Are you threatening me?" I asked.

"Let me put it this way," Bobby said, looking me straight in the eye. "Winning that game for the Giants was the greatest moment of my life. I'm not going to let you take it away from me. That's all I'm gonna say."

He had given me something to think about, that's for sure. I was torn. Maybe I should go back to 1951 to help Ralph and prevent Bobby from hitting the home run. Maybe I should help Bobby and just leave things alone. Or maybe I should do something so that *neither* of them would be a hero or a goat.

But if I did that, *both* of them would turn out to be nobodies. All that money they would eventually earn signing autographs together would vanish. I would be stealing money from *both* of them. I would be ruining *both* of their lives.

Is it right to tamper with history at *all*, I wondered? My thoughts were all jumbled in my head.

I remember reading about something called the "butterfly effect." It's pretty complicated, but it boils down to the theory that an insignificant little action—like the flapping of a butterfly's wings—could set off a series of events that would cause something really bizarre to happen. A butterfly could flap its wings in Ohio, and it might eventually cause a tornado in Hawaii. Every little moment of our lives might change what happens afterward.

For example, if my dad had driven just a *little* bit slower or a *little* bit faster on the day of his accident, he wouldn't have been hit by that drunk driver. He wouldn't be sitting in a wheelchair today. If the bullets that killed Presidents Kennedy and Lincoln had been a few inches to the left or right, those men would have lived and American history would be totally different.

And if Bobby Thomson had hit that ball just a fraction of an inch lower or higher on the bat, there never would have been a Shot Heard Round the World. Everything would have been different. He wouldn't be a hero. Ralph wouldn't be a goat. Nobody would have ever heard of either of them. It would be a different future. Maybe it would have been better. Maybe it would have been worse. And the Dodgers, most likely, would have won the pennant in 1951.

Sometimes the simplest thing changes everything. What if every little decision we make matters and changes things that will happen down the line?

My head was spinning. Messing with something that happened back in 1951 was too dangerous, I decided. I would not take the trip after all.

"I'll make a deal with you," I said to Bobby.

"What kind of deal?"

"I won't interfere with your home run," I told him. "But you've got to do something for me."

"What?"

I got out the plaque that my dad had given me for my birthday. I handed it to Bobby.

"Will you sign your card for me?" I asked.

"Sure, kid," he said, taking a pen off my night table. "If Branca signed his card, it's only right for me to sign mine, too."

As I went to sleep that night, things were looking good. I got *both* of the baseball cards signed, and I didn't even have to go back in time to do it.

That gave me an idea—now the plaque with the two cards was valuable. It might be worth a few thousand dollars. I could sell it and give my dad the money so he could start his business.

Everybody would be happy.

6

For the Fun of It

EVEN THOUGH BOTH OF THE BASEBALL CARDS WERE SIGNED and probably worth a lot of money, I was feeling a little depressed after my visit from Bobby Thomson. I didn't know exactly why.

Then, as I looked at Uncle Wilbur's old clothes hanging from my doorknob, I realized what it was. I *wanted* to go back to 1951. After getting permission from my mom and doing all that research and preparation, I was looking forward to this adventure. I felt like I was all dressed up with no place to go.

I pulled out the box score from the game, which I had photocopied at the library. A box score is an amazing little thing, when you think about it. Without a single sentence, it tells the whole story of a game, right down to the attendance and the names of the umpires. Sometimes I go to the library and dig up newspapers on microfilm just to read the box scores of baseball games from decades past.

I was struck by the names of the guys who played in this famous game. Stanky, Mays, Maglie, Irvin, and Dark on the Giants. Robinson, Reese, Snider, Furillo, Newcombe, and Hodges on the Dodgers. I knew those names better than I knew the names of guys who are playing Major League Baseball *today*. Half of them made it into the Hall of Fame. Then, of course, there were Bobby Thomson and Ralph Branca. And who could forget Leo Durocher, the famous manager of the Giants?

A thought popped into my head: What if I went back to 1951 and just *watched* the game?

Giants	AB.	R.	H.	O.	A.	E.
Stanky, 2b	4	0	0	0	4	0
Dark, ss	4	1	1	2	2	0
Mueller, rf	4	0	1	0	0	0
‡Hartung	0	1	0	0	0	0
Irvin, lf	4	1	1	1	0	0
Lockman, 1b	3	1	2	11	1	0
Thomson, 3b	4	1	3	4	1	0
Mays, cf	3	0	0	1	0	0
Westrum, c	0	0	0	7	1	0
*Rigney	1	0	0	0	0	0
Noble, c	0	0	0	0	0	0
Maglie, p	2	0	0	1	2	0
†Thompson	1	0	0	0	0	0
Jansen, p	0	0	0	0	0	0
Totals	30	5	8	27	11	0

Dodgers	AB.	R.	H.	O.	A.	E.
Furillo, rf	5	0	0	0	0	0
Reese, ss	4	2	1	2	5	0
Snider, cf	3	1	2	1	0	0
Robinson, 2b	2	1	1	3	2	0
Pafko, lf	4	0	1	4	1	0
Hodges, 1b	4	0	0	11	1	0
Cox, 3b	4	0	2	1	3	0
Walker, c	4	0	1	2	0	0
Newcombe, p	4	0	0	1	1	0
Branca, p	0	0	0	0	0	0
Totals	34	4	8	25	13	0

*Struck out for Westrum in eighth.
†Grounded out for Maglie in eighth.
‡Ran for Mueller in ninth.
§One out when winning run scored.

Dodgers ___ 1 0 0 0 0 0 0 3 0—4
Giants ___ 0 0 0 0 0 0 1 0 4—5

Runs batted in—Robinson, Thomson (4), Pafko, Cox, Lockman. Two base hits—Thomson, Irvin, Lockman. Home run—Thomson. Sacrifice hit—Lockman. Double plays — Cox, Robinson and Hodges; Reese, Robinson and Hodges. Bases on balls—Off Maglie, 4 (Reese, Snider, Robinson 2); Newcombe, 2 (Westrum 2). Struck out—By Maglie, 6 (Furillo, Walker 2, Snider, Pafko, Reese); Newcombe, 2 (Mays, Rigney). Pitching records—Off Maglie 8 hits, 4 runs in 8 innings; Jansen 0 hits, 0 runs in 1; Newcombe, 7 hits, 4 runs in 8½ innings; Branca, 1 hit, 1 run in 0 innings (pitched to one batter in ninth). Left on base—Dodgers, 7; Giants, 3. Earned runs—Giants, 5; Dodgers, 4. Wild pitch—Maglie. Winner—Jansen (23 - 11). Loser—Branca (13-12). Umpires—Jorda at plate, Conlan, first base; Stewart, second base; Goetz, third base. Time—2:28. Attendance—34,320.

October 3, 1951

Up until this point, whenever I traveled through time I always had some mission I hoped to accomplish. I wanted to see with my own eyes whether or not Babe Ruth *really* called his famous "called shot" home run. I wanted to stop Ted Williams from joining the Marines and missing four years of his baseball career. I wanted to prevent Roberto Clemente from getting on the plane that was going to crash and kill him. I always had an important reason to go back in time.

What if I had no mission at all? What was to prevent me from going back in time just for the *fun* of it? It would be cool to witness the Shot Heard Round the World—the most famous home run in baseball history.

I could be a spectator for a change. A tourist. I could just buy a ticket and walk into the ballpark like anybody else. Nobody would ever know. What would be the harm in that?

I decided to do it. I wouldn't try to interfere with the game at all. I'd just watch. This could be a little birthday present to myself.

It would be unwieldy to take my wooden plaque with the two cards on it back in time with me. What would I do with the plaque when I got to 1951? No, it would be smarter to take a card off the plaque and just bring that one card with me.

One problem—the cards were glued to the wood.

I tiptoed downstairs and rooted around until I found a single-edge razor blade and a pair of rubber gloves. I put on the gloves and carefully—very carefully— separated the Ralph Branca card from the wood. It wasn't easy. That thing had been in place for a long time, probably before collecting baseball cards became a popular hobby. Nobody in their right mind would glue cards to a wooden plaque today. They'd put them in a plastic holder.

It took about ten minutes of hard work to remove the card from the wood. It was in okay shape. Not mint, but okay. I gathered all the stuff my mom had put on my bed—the umbrella, the food, the Band-Aids, and so on.

I was ready. I knew that soon after I took off the rubber gloves and held the card in my hand, things would start happening. I'd get that tingling sensation in my fingertips.

But wait. I had the vague sense that I was forgetting something. After all the preparation I had done, something was missing. What was it? I searched my memory and scolded myself. I should have made a to-do list.

Oh yeah! A new pack of cards! Just as the 1951 Ralph Branca card was going to be my ticket to the past, I would need a *new* card to get me back to the present day. I went to my desk and fished through the drawers until I found an unopened pack of cards.

Whew! If I hadn't remembered that and went back to 1951 without it, I would have been stuck in the past for the rest of my life.

I gathered the stuff on my bed again and made myself comfortable. This wasn't scary. No, not anymore. I had done this so many times now that I wasn't afraid of what was going to happen. It was more anticipation.

No matter how much I had prepared, no matter

how much I had researched, it was impossible to predict exactly what was going to happen when I arrived
at the Polo Grounds. I would have to be ready for
anything.

I took a deep breath and removed the rubber
gloves. I picked up the Branca card in my right hand.
Closing my eyes, I thought about 1951. Mentally, I
willed myself *not* to think about the Korean War. I
didn't want to end up in Korea, that was for sure. I'd
already been there, with Ted Williams, and almost
got killed. No, I wanted to go to New York City.

Take me to 1951, I thought.

I fingered the money in my pocket that my mom
had given me. *Maybe I'll buy a candy bar when I get
to New York*, I thought. Back in 1951, you could get a
candy bar for a nickel. Everything was cheaper back
then. I could buy just about anything I wanted.

Soon, I had the sense that something was happening to me. The buzzy feeling came to my fingertips,
the way it always does. It was gentle at first, like a
cat purring, or a string on a guitar vibrating. It felt
nice.

I knew what was going to happen next. The tingling sensation was going to move, to spread. It went
from the tips of my right fingers up my hand, across
my wrist, and throughout my whole arm. I felt like
my arm had fallen asleep because I'd slept on it the
wrong way.

And then, while I was thinking about that, I felt
my whole chest vibrating. I had reached the point of

no return now. Even if I dropped the card at that moment, it was too late to reverse what I had started. I was going back in time whether I wanted to or not. I hoped that I hadn't screwed anything up in my preparation.

What if the Branca card wasn't really from 1951? What if I arrived in January instead of October? There were so many things that could go wrong.

Too late to worry about that stuff. My whole body was tingling now. What a feeling! Suddenly it was like I was twenty pounds lighter, and then *fifty* pounds lighter. It was as if I was becoming weightless. I felt like I could just rise up off the bed like a balloon and float around the room, the way astronauts do in zero gravity. That's how light I felt.

I fought the temptation to open my eyes and watch what I knew was going to happen next. It would be so cool to watch myself disappear, but maybe a little frightening at the same time. So I kept my eyes closed.

Take me to 1951, I kept repeating to myself. *Take me to 1951.*

And then, I vanished.

You Only Live Once

WHEN I OPENED MY EYES, I WAS HIT BY A BLAST OF BRIGHT sunlight that forced me to squint and turn my head away. It was morning, that was for sure. I could tell by the angle of the sun in the sky. It was probably around nine o'clock, maybe even earlier.

I checked to see if all my body parts were in the right places, and that I had all the stuff I had brought with me. Check, check, check. Nothing missing.

I looked around. Ticket booths. Gate D. So far, so good. I was at the Polo Grounds.

The Branca card was still in my hand, luckily. It was worth a lot of money, and I didn't want to lose it. I slipped it into my shirt pocket for safe-keeping. The umbrella and the other stuff, I didn't need. I left it all on a bench for somebody else to pick up. Mom might be mad, but I like to travel light. I'd tell her I lost it.

For once in my life, it looked like I had landed *exactly* where I wanted to be. Usually, when I went back in time, I landed someplace *near* where I wanted to be. Then I had to find the way to my destination. Time travel would probably never be an exact science. But this time, things were looking better than usual.

There weren't any people around, but that didn't surprise me. Day games usually start around one o'clock in the afternoon. The players wouldn't be arriving for a few hours. I knew that they had night games in 1951, but most baseball games still took place during the day.

I was pretty sure I had the right year, but I wanted to make sure I had arrived on the right *day*. The easiest way to find out was to look at a newspaper.

There weren't any newsstands around, but there was the next best thing—a garbage can. You can almost always find a newspaper in a garbage can, especially back in the old days before they had recycling.

I spotted a can near the corner and went over to it. I rooted around until I found a copy of the *New York Times*. . . .

$\mathfrak{New\ York\ Ti}$

The New York Times Company

NEW YORK, TUESDAY, OCTOBER 2, 1951.

Okay, good. It was probably yesterday's paper. Everything was working out perfectly. After eleven trips, I was finally getting the hang of this time travel thing. Maybe my luck had finally changed.

I scanned the *Times* for a minute. It cost just five cents in 1951, I noticed. The first parking meters were being installed in Brooklyn. The heavyweight champion Joe Louis had signed a contract to fight Rocky Marciano. RCA was inviting the public to see an early test of color television. But I wasn't about to waste my time reading the paper. I wanted to get inside the ballpark.

Standing right next to it, I thought the Polo Grounds somehow looked different from the other times I had been there. I pulled on a door, but it was locked. I tried another one. No luck. I looked for a window I might be able to climb into. But it was a solid brick wall. It occurred to me that maybe I was in the *back* of the ballpark. I walked all the way around to the front and backed away from the wall until I saw this. . . .

What?! Yankee Stadium isn't even in Manhattan. It's in the *Bronx*. Everybody knows that. That's why the Yankees are called "The Bronx Bombers." I needed to be in Manhattan. What was I doing *here*? Somehow, I had messed up, again.

Across the street, I spotted a guy in overalls pushing a big broom. He was on a walkway next to the river. I ran over to him.

"Excuse me," I said in my most polite voice. "Can you tell me how to get to the Polo Grounds?"

The guy stopped sweeping and looked up at me with disgust.

"You from outta town?" he asked me. "Or just stupid?"

He turned around and pointed across the river. There was a ballpark on the other side, and a big hill behind it.

I didn't know that the Polo Grounds and Yankee Stadium were so close to each other.

Of *course*! Yankee Stadium and the Polo Grounds were right *next* to each other on either side of the Harlem River. I *knew* that. I had forgotten.

"I'm from out of town," I said, running off. "Thanks, mister!"

"Fuhgetaboutit," he mumbled.

One of the things I like about New York City is that it's easy to get around, because the streets are numbered. There was a small bridge that crossed

over the Harlem River into Manhattan. A little sign
said it was the Macombs Dam Bridge, and it opened
in 1895. That was the year Babe Ruth was born, I
remembered. I jogged across the bridge.

It ended with a fork that led onto 155th Street.
I walked two blocks north to 157th, and there it
was. . . .

The Polo Grounds.

It wasn't a beautiful ballpark, like Wrigley Field,
Shibe Park, and some of the other places I had visited. But *this* was the ballpark I remembered from
my previous trips. I ran across the street and peered
through the chain-link fence. The place looked
empty.

I figured I would just hang out at the front gate
until somebody showed up and the ticket booths
opened. There was a lot of time to kill. I wished I had
brought a portable video game system, or something
to read. Waiting is boring.

That's when I remembered the little video camera
that my grandmother had given me for my birthday.
I had been planning to bring it along and shoot some
video from 1951, but I must have left it on the desk in
my room. Bummer!

I kept looking through the fence and thinking
that *anybody* could sneak into this place. There
were no surveillance cameras or anything. They
really should have some security. Any lunatic
could waltz right into the Polo Grounds and plant

a bomb, start a fire, or who knows what? I guess they didn't have to worry about terrorism and stuff like that back in 1951.

Eventually, I got tired of waiting. YOLO, right? You only live once. I dug my sneaker in and hopped the fence. If anybody stopped me, I figured, I would just play dumb and buy a ticket later. I had the money my mom had given me.

But nobody stopped me. Nobody was around. Not even the groundskeeper. I had the run of the place. It was like a ghost town. I hopped another fence inside and a few seconds later I was climbing over a short wall near the third-base line to get right on the field.

Have you ever been in a ballpark all by yourself? It's sort of an eerie, beautiful feeling. I felt like a neutron bomb had wiped out the human race, and I was the only living person left on Earth.

I ran out to second base and spun around slowly to see the Polo Grounds as a panorama. I pinched myself to make sure it was real. Here I was, standing in a place that didn't exist anymore. I knew the Polo Grounds had been torn down in the 1960s. In my time, there was an apartment building complex on the site. For that matter, Yankee Stadium had been torn down, too. But that was just a few years ago. Neither of these great ballparks was with us anymore. Probably most of the buildings from 1951 had been torn down a long time ago.

**At the Polo Grounds, the center-field wall was
nearly twice as far as the foul lines.**

The Polo Grounds was pretty much the way I
remembered it from my previous trips. It's shaped
like a giant horseshoe, with the open end at center
field. It was actually possible to hit a home run that
traveled only 260 feet down the foul lines, and yet
you could blast a shot 450 feet to center field that
would be a fly ball out. It didn't seem fair.

There was a huge sign over the scoreboard—an
ad for Chesterfield with a giant cigarette on it.
REGULAR & KING-SIZE, it said. A HIT!

So much history had taken place on this field.

And I'm not just talking about all the famous base-ball and football games that were played here. I had read somewhere on the internet that the hot dog was invented in the Polo Grounds in 1900. That's right. Some sausage salesman ran out of plates during a game, so he started wrapping his sausages in rolls. For all I know, that could be one of those urban legends. You never know how much truth there is to these stories.

I do know *this*: In 1908, a guy named Jack Nor-worth was riding the New York subway when he saw an ad for a Giants game at the Polo Grounds. Nor-worth had never been to a baseball game in his life. But the ad inspired him to write a little song you may have heard of—"Take Me Out to the Ball Game."

That's a true story. You can look it up if you don't believe me.

I jogged over to the batter's box and took a couple of pretend swings. This was the exact spot, I remembered, where Ray Chapman of the Cleveland Indians was standing when a fastball from Carl Mays shattered his skull. Chapman died a few hours later. It was the only time in baseball history when a batter was killed by a pitched ball. Of course, that was in 1920, before they had batting helmets.

I looked toward the outfield. Everything was green—the grass, the wall, even the seats were painted green. A green background, I knew, makes it easier for batters to see the ball.

The upper deck stuck out about ten feet over the

lower deck. On the wall out in left field was the number 315. *That's where Thomson is going to hit the Shot Heard Round the World*, I remembered from my research.

The left and right field lines were *really* short. I could probably hit a ball *that* far. But on the wall out in center field was the number 483. *Four hundred and eighty-three feet.* That's a *long* way to hit a baseball. It looked like center field went on forever.

I remembered a photo of Willie Mays making a spectacular on-the-run, over-the-shoulder catch out there during the 1954 World Series. It was so famous that it came to be called "the Catch."

I can't imagine how Willie ever caught up with that ball.

I jogged out to center field to re-create Willie's famous play. A few feet to the left of where he caught the ball, above the center field wall, were two bronze plaques. I went over to see what they said. One was in honor of a guy named Eddie Grant. I had never heard of him, but the plaque said he played for the Giants, and he was the first major league player to be killed fighting in World War I. The other plaque was a monument to the Hall of Fame Giant pitcher Christy Mathewson. I had met him when I went to visit Jim Thorpe in 1913. It read . . .

THE GREATEST PITCHER OF HIS ERA
AND ONE OF THE FINEST SPORTSMEN
OF ALL TIME. FOR HIS MODE OF LIFE
AND CONDUCT AT ALL TIMES, HE
STOOD FORTH AS AN EXAMPLE TO HIS
FELLOW PLAYERS.

Directly above the plaque was a row of seven windows. There were wire screens covering them, I suppose to prevent a home-run shot from shattering the glass. I couldn't imagine anyone hitting a ball that far, but you never know.

I had to go to the bathroom, and I figured there must be one behind those windows. There was a staircase near the big scoreboard. It looked like the stairs led up behind the windows, so I climbed up two flights of steps.

I was right. There were no fancy hand dryers or

automatic paper towel dispensers in the bathroom, but at least it was clean. I did my business and as I left, I noticed that there was a whole complex of offices up there, three stories above center field. There was a trainer's room, with whirlpool tubs and massage tables. The door was wide open. There was also a supply room filled with bats and balls and other equipment. There was a laundry room. That must be where they clean the uniforms after every game.

Next to the laundry room was the Giants' locker room. For a moment, it crossed my mind that I shouldn't be in here snooping around, but my curiosity got the better of me. How often does a kid get an opportunity to peek in a major league locker room? Not often. And how often does a kid get an opportunity to peek in a major league locker room that was torn down over sixty years ago? Never.

I looked at the names written on tape over the lockers—Mays, Maglie, Irvin, Thomson. I was kicking myself for not remembering to bring my new video camera with me.

There was a sign on the wall of the locker room. . . .

WHAT YOU HEAR HERE,
WHAT YOU SEE HERE,
AND WHAT YOU SAY HERE
MUST STAY HERE.

Next to the locker room was a green door that

said MANAGER'S OFFICE. I couldn't resist. I had to peek inside. Leo Durocher was one of the most famous managers in baseball history. I flipped on the light.

It was a surprisingly small room, with a wooden coat tree and a bunch of clipboards hanging from hooks on one wall. There was a leather swivel chair in front of a wooden desk with glass top. There were some framed photos on the desk—Durocher and his wife, a team photo, a picture of Franklin Roosevelt smoking a cigarette. The desk faced a big window that looked out on the field. I realized that I was a few feet above that Christy Mathewson plaque I had seen in straightaway center field.

Then I noticed something odd. Right next to the desk was a telescope.

I went over to have a look. It was a nice one, maybe two feet long, extended. It had four collapsing sections, one of them black grain leather. Another section had the word WOLLENSAK engraved in it.

It was right next to the desk, on a tripod.

The telescope was on a tripod, and pointing out the window. There was a small cutaway in the wire mesh that covered the window, obviously so the person looking through the telescope could see better.

I leaned over and looked through the eyepiece. Wow, the thing was *powerful*. The telescope was pointed at home plate, which just about filled the lens. You could get a really good view from this spot. I felt like I was right on top of the action.

At this point, I probably should have put two and two together. But I didn't. Not yet. I figured Durocher just used the telescope to get a better view of the game. But managers don't watch the game from center field. They sit in the dugout.

Then I noticed something else. On the desk, right next to the telescope, was a button. It looked sort of like a doorbell.

Huh! Why would somebody have a doorbell mounted on their desk? That didn't make any sense.

I pushed the button. Off in the distance, there was a faint buzz. I pushed the button again. *Bzzzz.* Every time I pushed the button, the buzzer sounded. I could hear it because the ballpark was deserted. If it was filled up with fans, I never would have been able to hear the buzzer.

I sat back in Durocher's chair and slapped my forehead. It didn't take any genius to figure out what was going on. Leo Durocher had somebody hiding in his office during games, peering through the telescope. They could spy on the opposing catcher's signs to the pitcher.

The wires to the buzzer system probably led to

the Giants' bullpen, which I could see was halfway down the foul line. The guy looking through the telescope could use the buzzer to indicate whether the next pitch was going to be a fastball, a curveball, or whatever. Then, somebody in the bullpen could signal the batter to let him know what pitch was coming next.

Wow! That guy at the baseball card show who sold us the plaque was *right*.

The Giants *were* cheating.

The Right Thing to Do

THERE'S NOTHING WRONG WITH STEALING SIGNS. IT'S PER-
fectly legal in baseball. Even in my league in
Louisville, we steal signs all the time. Flip always
tells us that if we reach second base, we should watch
the catcher carefully. If we see how many fingers he's
putting down, and it's just one for a fastball and two
for a curve, we can let our hitter know which pitch is
coming next.

Knowing what the pitcher's going to throw is a
big advantage. I know that I would hit a lot better if
I knew in advance whether the pitcher was going to
throw me a fastball or a curve.

Stealing signs is not only legal, it's a badge of
honor if you can pull it off. It's also one of those things
that makes the game so fascinating. The average fan
doesn't even know it's going on, but the people who
understand the game well really get into the science

of sign stealing. It's like espionage.

But it's one thing to steal signs with your naked eye. It's another to hide a telescope in the outfield and relay the stolen signs using an electric buzzer system. I'm pretty sure that's against the rules. It's also just not fair, because only the home team is able to take advantage of it.

My mind was racing. As I sat there in Leo Durocher's leather chair, I realized that this changed *everything*.

Poor Ralph Branca had to live his whole life as baseball's biggest goat because he threw the pitch that Thomson hit for the Shot Heard Round the World. But now I knew the truth. Bobby Thomson probably knew in advance which pitch was coming. If the Giants hadn't been stealing signs illegally, he never would have hit that home run.

Heck, if the Giants hadn't been stealing signs illegally, there might never have *been* a playoff in the first place. They never would have come from behind and caught up with the Dodgers during the last weeks of the season. Most likely, they won at least some of those games in the final days of the pennant race because they cheated.

My plan had been just to watch the game as a spectator, but not anymore.

I felt like I had to do something to make things right. I had to help Branca and the Dodgers. I could right a wrong. I was the only person who could do it, and I was in the perfect position.

But what could I do? What could I do to prevent Thomson from hitting that home run? I thought about my options.

Maybe I could tamper with Thomson's bat, I thought. But that would be hard to do, and who knows what might happen if I got caught. It might not matter, either. Bobby could just as easily hit the home run with a *different* bat if he knew what pitch was coming.

What if I busted the telescope so the Giants couldn't use it? No, destroying property is wrong. Two wrongs don't make a right.

I looked at the clock on Leo Durocher's wall. It was ten o'clock now. Time was getting short. Soon the players would start to arrive at the ballpark. I was going to have to get out of Durocher's office.

I tried to think of another plan. Maybe I could go buy a ticket, sit in the stands, and wait until the moment Branca was about to throw the pitch. Then I could cause a disturbance of some sort to throw off Thomson's timing. No, with thousands of people in the stands, I might not even be heard.

I looked at the telescope again. The eyepiece was a separate section from the rest of it. I turned it, and saw that it was loose enough to unscrew. It was simple. A telescope can't work without an eyepiece. I could just take it off. Then the game would be played fair and square. Sports should be played on an "even playing field," as they say. Let the better team win, not the team that cheats.

Unscrewing the eyepiece wasn't as bad as busting the telescope. It still might be the wrong thing to do, but it wasn't quite *as* wrong. And because I was righting a wrong, it actually could be the right thing to do. It was a good solution. And it was an easy solution. At least that's what I convinced myself. I took off the eyepiece and slipped it into my pocket. Then I got up to leave.

That's when the door opened.

"Not so fast!" somebody shouted.

9

Baseball Is a War

I wheeled around. There were three guys standing in front of me. Two of them were wearing Giants uniforms, with the words NEW YORK stitched across their chests in black with orange trim. The guy in the middle was wearing a fancy suit with wide lapels and the kind of hat guys used to wear in the old days. None of them was smiling. The player on the left was holding a bat.

"Who are *you*?" the guy in the suit asked menacingly.

"I . . . I . . . I . . ."

I backed against the desk, hard. One of the framed photos toppled over. I could tell right away that the guy in the suit was Leo Durocher, the manager of the Giants. He looked older than the two players. I had seen lots of pictures of him. I knew that under that hat he was balding, and he slicked back what hair he had left. It had to be him. I was in his office.

Leo Durocher

"What are you doing here, kid?" Durocher snarled.

He was the kind of guy who could barely say a sentence without cursing. He looked like a gangster. His blue eyes were fiery. Veins were sticking out on his neck. I felt my heart beating in my chest. I had messed up, again. Why did I always mess up?

"The d-door wasn't locked," I stammered, trying desperately to think of something to say that would get me out of there. "I just opened it. . . ."

"Want me to bust his face, Leo?" asked the guy with the bat.

"I'll take care of this, Brat," said Durocher.

Brat. The guy with the bat had to be Eddie Stanky.

The second baseman. His nickname was "the Brat." I had read about him in a little paperback book I found at Flip's store one day. Stanky wasn't a great player, but he was known for doing *anything* to get on base, including getting hit by the ball. In the field, Stanky would jump around and wave his arms to distract opposing hitters.

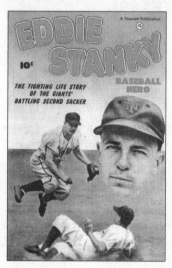

I had seen a book about Stanky in Flip's store.

He was a little guy, not much taller than me. But a baseball bat tends to make you look a lot tougher. Stanky pounded the barrel against the palm of his hand. He looked like he really wanted to bust my face.

The third guy hadn't said a word. I didn't know who he was. I looked around for an escape route.

"Who sent you here?" Durocher snapped, stepping

forward to stick his face close to mine. I could smell his breath. "Dressen?"

"I'm not dressing," I said. "I was just—"

"No, you *dope!*" Durocher interrupted me. "Charlie Dressen, the manager of the Dodgers. Did he send you here to spy on us?"

I thought about saying yes. Maybe it would get me off the hook if I could blame it on somebody else. But I couldn't bring myself to do that.

"No!" I replied. "Nobody sent me. I sent myself."

The third guy, the quiet one, finally opened up his mouth.

"Maybe *we'll* send you someplace, kid. Someplace where nobody will find you for a *long* time."

"Shut up, Sal," said Durocher. "Don't be stupid."

Sal "the Barber" Maglie

Sal. That had to be Sal Maglie, the pitcher. They used to call him "the Barber" because he liked to throw at batters' chins and knock them down. It also looked like he hadn't shaved in a few days. He had a five o'clock shadow. All three of them looked like mean guys, like bad guys in cowboy movies. I couldn't imagine any of them ever smiling.

This was not good. I had been in a situation like this once before, I remembered. It was the time I went back to 1919 trying to prevent the Black Sox Scandal from happening and save the career of Shoeless Joe Jackson. I got caught by some gamblers who were trying to "fix" the World Series. They tied me to a chair and actually *shot* me. It was a miracle that I got out of that one alive.

I didn't think these guys were going to shoot me. They weren't criminals. In a worst-case scenario, I figured, they might beat me up pretty bad. Or they could just call the police and have me arrested for trespassing. That wouldn't be good. But they had caught me red-handed in Leo Durocher's office.

Of course, I had caught *them* red-handed, too. That was my only advantage. I touched my pocket to make sure I still had the eyepiece.

"What are you doing with that telescope?" I asked Durocher.

In retrospect, it was a dumb thing to say. But when you get caught by three guys in a place you shouldn't be, and one of them is menacing you with a bat, you tend to say dumb things. Whatever they were going to do to me, they were going to do to me no matter what. I had nothing to lose.

I shot a glance around the office. The window had that wire mesh over it. I wasn't going to be escaping that way. The door was still open.

"*I'll* ask the questions around here, kid," Durocher barked, his hot breath in my face. "This is *my* office. You got no business being in here. This place is private. I could call the cops on you."

"You're cheating," I said, pointing my finger at him. "You're not playing by the rules."

At that point, Durocher took a step back away from me. A little smile crept across his face. But it wasn't a happy smile. It was sort of a sneering smile that you have when you just beat your worst enemy.

"I'll tell you what I'm doing with the telescope," Durocher said. "I like lookin' at the stars. It relaxes me before a big game."

Maglie and Stanky laughed. Durocher told them to knock it off.

"If you're looking up at the stars, then why is the telescope pointing a few inches above home plate?" I asked. "There are no stars at home plate. You're stealing signs and using a buzzer system to tip off your batters which pitch is coming next."

"That's a load of crap!" Stanky shouted.

"Calm down, Eddie," Durocher said, turning to face Stanky. "He's a smart kid. I'm sure he'll listen to reason."

Maybe he was going to offer me money or an

autographed baseball to keep quiet, I thought for a moment. That would be nice.

Nah, if he wanted to keep me quiet, it would be easier for him to beat me up and threaten me with something worse.

In the moment Durocher was facing away from me, I thought I saw an opening. Maglie was looking at Durocher, and there was about two feet of open space between him and a file cabinet. If I could make it through that opening, I might be able to get out the door before they caught me. If I could find my way through the hallways to the center-field bleachers, I would be in the clear. They wouldn't want to be seen chasing a kid through the stands. The only thing I had going for me was the element of surprise.

So I made a run for it.

"Grab him, boys!" Durocher shouted.

Maglie dove at me like a football player making a tackle. He managed to grab one of my ankles. I tripped and went down before I got to the door. Stanky piled on top of me, just to be sure I couldn't get away. The two of them were crushing me. My nose was pressed against the cold floor.

"Oh, he's a squirmy one, this kid," Maglie grunted, twisting my arm behind my back.

"Owww!" I moaned.

"Pick him up, boys," Durocher ordered. Now he was *really* mad.

Maglie and Stanky grabbed my arms roughly and yanked me to my feet. They were holding me tight.

"Owww! That *hurts*!" I shouted. "I won't tell anybody! I promise! I'll pretend I didn't see anything."

"I don't trust you, kid," Durocher said.

He went over and closed the door to make sure that I couldn't make another break for it. It would muffle the sound if I started screaming, too. Then he stuck his face next to mine again.

"Do you know how many years it's been since this team won a pennant, kid?" Durocher asked me.

I didn't know. But he didn't wait for my answer anyway.

"Thirteen years," said Durocher. "That's a *long* time. I don't like to lose, son. My boys have come a long way this year. We started the season lousy. We were thirteen and a half games behind the Dodgers with just forty-four left to play. But we fought, and we scratched, and we clawed to get where we are right now. Tied for first place. And if we win today, it'll all be worth it."

"That won't make it right," I told him. "You cheated. How can you sleep at night? You stole signs. That's the only reason you came from behind and caught the Dodgers. Without the telescope, your season would have been over weeks ago."

"Oh yeah?" Durocher shot back in my face. "Are you too young to remember the war, kid? We decoded secret messages sent by the Japanese and Germans. We used our technology and our intelligence to steal *their* signs. That's how we won. Was *that* cheating? What's the difference now, kid?"

"It's not the same thing," I told him. "Hitler was trying to take over the world. That was a war."

"*Baseball* is a war, kid," he said, "and I say you win any way you can as long as you can get away with it. And we're gonna get away with it."

There was no point in arguing with him. I remembered the name of his autobiography, which I had seen on the shelves at the library—*Nice Guys Finish Last*.

"What are you gonna do to me?" I asked, expecting the worst. I felt sweat dripping down my armpits.

"Good question," Durocher said. "Boys? What do you think we should do with this kid?"

"We can't let him blab, Leo," Stanky said, tightening his grip on my arm. "We've come too far to have some punk kid mess everything up now."

"We could throw him out on the street," Maglie said. "Or call the cops."

"Nah, he could still squawk," Durocher said. "We can't let him go."

"Break his legs," Stanky suggested. "That'll shut him up."

I thought I was going to faint.

"Nah," said Durocher. "We gotta take him somewhere and keep him quiet, at least until the game's over."

"We don't have a lot of time," Maglie said. "I gotta go warm up."

Durocher snapped his fingers.

"I have an idea," he said. "Follow me."

He opened the door and made a right turn down the hallway, the same hallway I had walked down to get into his office. Stanky and Maglie dragged me by my arms. There was no use struggling. They were stronger than me, and there were two of them.

"Stop! Let me go!" I shouted. I started to scream, but Stanky put his hand over my face to muffle the sound. I tried to bite him. He shoved the bat in my mouth.

Durocher stopped at the equipment room and yanked open the door. The other two dragged me into the room. The door closed behind us. It smelled musty.

"Tie him to the chair," Durocher ordered Stanky and Maglie.

Oh no, not *again*.

They shoved me down onto a wooden folding chair. Durocher stood back and watched as the other two took some rope off a shelf and started tying me up with it. It didn't look like they had a lot of experience tying people up, and they fumbled with the rope. Durocher was impatient.

"Hurry up!"

While they worked on the ropes, I looked around the little equipment room. One bare light bulb dangled down from the ceiling on a wire. The shelves were filled with baseball caps, rosin bags, tubes of pine tar, boxes of jockstraps, and other baseball paraphernalia. I tried to take it all in. If I could get out of the ropes, some of this stuff might come in handy.

"Are you going to kill me?" I asked.

"If you don't shut up we will," Durocher told me. "You ask too many questions, you know that, kid?"

Stanky and Maglie were almost finished tying my arms and legs to the chair. They weren't sailors, but the ropes were reasonably secure.

"Better pat him down," Maglie said, "to make sure he doesn't have a knife or something."

I prayed that they wouldn't find the eyepiece from the telescope in my pants pocket. Or my pack of new cards. That would be the *worst* thing to happen. If I lost those, I'd be stuck in 1951 forever.

They didn't pat me down very well, and they didn't find the eyepiece or my pack of cards. What they *did* find was the Ralph Branca baseball card in my shirt pocket. That was the card I'd used to get back to 1951.

"Well, well, well, what's *this*?" Durocher said as he looked at the card. "You're a Dodger fan! That figures. So you *are* spying on us for them."

"I am not!" I protested. "I'm just a fan."

"I see your pal Branca even signed the card for you," Durocher said. "You must love the Dodgers. Well, you know what you can do with *this*."

With that, Durocher pinched my Branca card between his fingers and ripped it in half. Then he laughed, ripped it into quarters, and flipped them in the air like confetti.

"No!" I shouted as the pieces of cardboard fluttered to the floor.

"That card was worth a hundred bucks!" I shouted. "Maybe more. You didn't have to do that."

"A hundred bucks?" Maglie said. The three of them cackled as if that was the funniest thing they'd ever heard.

"You're a real comedian, kid," Durocher said. "Too bad we can't let you hang around and tell us some more jokes."

He pulled a T-shirt off the shelf and ripped it to make a long strip of cloth. Then he tied it around my head tightly, so that the cloth was jammed in my mouth. He put another T-shirt over my head.

"Just to make sure you don't get any ideas about screaming for help," he said.

"Let's get outta here," Maglie said. "We can deal with the kid after the game."

"After we win the pennant," Stanky added.

The three of them went out the door. Just before it closed, Durocher came back, as if he'd forgotten something.

He turned off the light.

"Enjoy the game," he said.

Then he left, slamming the door behind him.

10

Trapped

TOTAL DARKNESS.

Why does this always have to happen to *me*?

I was kicking myself. I couldn't believe that I had screwed up *again*. Why can't everything go smoothly, just once? No matter how carefully I plan things out, whenever I go back in time, something goes wrong.

It occurred to me that maybe I shouldn't do any planning at all. I should just wing it. I'd probably be better off. I couldn't be any *worse* off, that was for sure.

Desperately, I pulled on the ropes that were binding my arms and legs to the chair. They weren't tied expertly, but there were a lot of them and I couldn't get them loose. I might have made things worse for myself by making the knots tighter. I pulled until I was out of breath and I felt my heart beating fast.

I tried to twist my head all around and to bite

the cloth over my mouth, but I couldn't get it off. I couldn't yell for help. I tried to rock the chair back and forth. It may have been possible to topple it over, but that seemed like a bad idea, because it would be so easy for my head to hit the floor when I fell.

There was nothing to do but sit there. I was stuck. I felt tears welling up in my eyes. I was so stupid.

After my eyes had adjusted to the dark, I thought I could see a sliver of light under the door. I *hoped* there was an opening there. If not, I might run out of air. Maybe I was just hallucinating. My arms and legs were sore from pulling against the ropes.

Still, I was grateful just to be alive. Leo Durocher and his henchmen could have tortured me, burned me, or killed me. Who knew what those guys were capable of doing in order to win the pennant?

This is it, I said to myself. This is the last time I would travel through time. My mom was right. It's just too dangerous. There are too many things that can go wrong.

I was lucky Durocher and his boys hadn't found my pack of new baseball cards in my back pocket. Without them, I would be stuck in 1951. Stuck in the past forever.

I didn't know how much time had passed since they locked me in the equipment room. I may have fallen asleep at some point. I wasn't sure. It could have been hours, or it could have been twenty minutes. I thought I heard some cheering at one point. It could have been another sound. It was hard to tell.

The Giants may have had another eyepiece for the telescope, I figured. Maybe the game was over. Maybe the pennant was already won.

There was a sound outside the door. Footsteps, and then a hand on the doorknob. Oh, no, they were back! I prepared myself for the worst. The door opened. I squinted from the bright light.

"Don't kill me!" I tried to shout through the cloth over my face. "I won't say anything!"

The light flipped on and the cloth was pulled off. There was a guy standing in front of me. An African-American guy. He was a kid, really. He wasn't much taller than me, and he couldn't have been more than twenty years old. He was wearing regular clothes with a light gray sports jacket. He looked like he had seen a ghost.

"Say hey!" he said in a high-pitched, sort of squeaky voice. "What are *you* doing in here? You shouldn't be in here."

I tried to tell him what happened, but the gag in my mouth muffled my voice. He went behind me and untied the knot at the back of my head. The gag fell away. My jaw hurt, but it felt good to be able to communicate.

"Thank you!"

"Who did this to you?" the guy asked.

"Leo Durocher," I told him. "And Stanky. And Maglie. They brought me here and tied me up."

"That wasn't a very nice thing to do," he said as he started working on the knots that were binding my hands. "I'm sure Mr. Leo must have mistaken you for somebody else. He's a good man at heart. I'm going to talk to him about this. Yes sirree. He shouldn't be doing this to people. That's just not right."

"Oh, don't talk to him!" I said urgently. "If you could just let me out of here, I'd be so grateful. I can't thank you enough."

"No problem," he said. He untied the last knot that was holding my right wrist down. It was such a relief to be able to lift my arm off the chair.

"Who *are* you?" I asked him. "The bat boy?"

"No sir," he said, laughing a little. "I play ball for the Giants. You probably haven't heard of me. My name is Willie Mays."

Willie Mays

Wait a minute. *What?* For a moment, I thought I heard him wrong. Willie Mays? *The* Willie Mays?

I studied his face more closely as he worked on my other wrist. It *was* Willie Mays!

The great Willie Mays—very possibly the best all-around player in the history of the game—was on his knees in front of me, untying the ropes that held me to the chair. I couldn't believe it.

I knew all about Willie Mays, of course. What baseball fan didn't know his name? I had just about memorized his whole career. He hit 660 home runs. He was the National League MVP in 1954 and 1965. He also won twelve Gold Glove Awards, in a *row*. He was a Hall of Famer—a five-tool player, as they call the ones who can do it all. And most people don't know

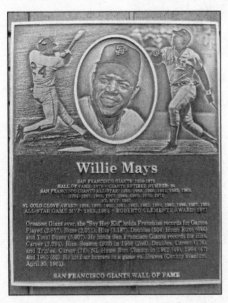

this fact about Willie Mays—he was the only player in history to hit four home runs in a game *and* three triples in a game. You could look it up.

Most of the pictures I had seen of Mays showed him when he was older, as an established star or a retired player. I thought of him as an old man. But in 1951,

I realized, Willie was in his rookie season. His career was just getting started. He looked so young, more boy than man.

Willie's forehead was sweating while he worked on freeing me from the ropes. Finally, he got the last knot loosened and I was able to stand up. Willie tossed all the rope off to the side. He shook my hand and I didn't want to let it go. I thanked him over and over again.

The door was open, and Durocher and his boys could come back at any minute. The smart thing to do would be to run out of there. But I was still in awe of the fact that I was in the presence of the great Willie Mays, before he was great. It was tempting to ask him for an autograph, but I didn't have a pencil or paper on me.

"Is the game over?" I asked him. "Did the Giants win the pennant?"

"The game didn't start yet," Willie told me. "I just came in here to think for a few minutes."

"Think?" I asked him. "Think about what?"

Willie sighed and sat on the chair I had been tied to.

"Stuff," he said. "The game. The pitcher. What I'm gonna do. I just needed to be by myself for a while. To clear my head, y'know? I come in here sometimes. Usually nobody's around."

Willie looked nervous and afraid. I actually thought he might break down in tears. I didn't know if I should leave him there.

"Are you gonna be okay?" I asked him.

"This is the biggest game of my life," he said, in a whisper. "Somebody's gonna win the pennant today. Somebody's gonna lose. And somebody's gonna get the blame. I just don't want to mess up in front of all those people. It's gonna be on TV coast-to-coast, y'know."

"You're going to be great," I told him, which was an understatement.

The fact was, I had no idea how Willie was going to do in the game. I had studied the box score, but I was concentrating on Ralph Branca and Bobby Thomson. The only thing I remembered about Willie Mays was what that baseball card dealer had told me—Willie was on deck when Thomson hit the Shot Heard Round the World.

"I don't know about that," Willie said as he wiped his forehead with the sleeve of his shirt. "I got the jitters. Since September first, I'm hitting .223. Maybe I'm not good enough to hit big league pitching. Maybe Mr. Leo is gonna send me back to the minors next season. I just hope I don't have to come to bat with the game on the line. Can't take that pressure."

Willie was terrified that he was going to flop in the majors and he'd have to go back home to Alabama and get a job in the laundry business. That's what he'd been training for in high school. He told me that his father was a sharecropper, and his parents had separated when he was three years old. His childhood was not an easy one.

"You won't come to bat with the game on the line," I assured him. "Don't worry. You're going to be on deck when the game ends."

Willie looked at me, puzzled.

"How do you know?" he asked. "How could anybody possibly know that?"

"I'm going to tell you a secret," I whispered. "You don't have to believe me if you don't want to. It's gonna sound crazy, I know. But I can travel through time. I live in the twenty-first century. I know *exactly* what's going to happen in this game, Willie. Bobby Thomson will be the last batter. You'll be in the on-deck circle when the game ends. That's all I can tell you."

Willie looked at me. Then a wide grin spread across his face.

"You're crazy!" he said, laughing. "You're a crazy boy!"

"Trust me," I told him. "You won't come to bat with the game on the line. You can relax."

Then I said good-bye to Willie, thanked him for helping me, and hightailed it out of there.

11

The Butterfly Effect

I RAN DOWN THE HALLWAY UNTIL I SAW A DOOR WITH AN exit sign over it, and I yanked it open. The important thing was to avoid anyone wearing a Giants uniform, except for Willie Mays, of course. If it hadn't been for Willie, who knows how long I would have been stuck in that room?

There were steps leading down. I took them two at a time. At the bottom was another hallway, and I caught a glimpse of green to my right—the field. I headed for it.

Fans were streaming into the ballpark now to watch batting practice. The stands were filling up. It was easy for me to blend into the crowd. I made my way around the perimeter of the field.

With both teams from New York, there was a mixture of Dodger fans and Giants fans in the stands. They were already chowing down on hot

dogs, popcorn, and beer. The smell of roasted peanuts was everywhere. Back home, peanuts come in
sealed plastic bags. It's just not the same.

"Newk's gonna mow 'em down today," some guy
wearing a Dodger cap said.

"No way. I say he don't make it past the fifth
inning. Giants all the way."

"You don't know nothin'."

"Fuhgetaboutit."

The air was damp and the sky had become over-
cast. It looked like it might rain. I glanced at the
American flag in center field over Leo Durocher's
office. The wind was blowing out to right. I over-
heard some lady say that Frank Sinatra might be at
the game, and she was all excited to see him.

Behind the plate, some guys were setting up a
huge TV camera on a tripod. It had the NBC logo
on the side. Willie was right. I remembered reading at the library that this was the first series
to be broadcast live to a national TV audience.
Around sixteen million people would be watching
the game. That's just about everybody who *owned*
a TV in 1951.

Directly above my head, I could see the press box.
There was a line of reporters sitting up there, maybe
fifty of them. All men, and they were all smoking
cigarettes and wearing those old-time fedora hats
like the one Leo Durocher had had on. Each reporter
had a typewriter in front of him. It occurred to me
that those were three things I had never seen in a

twenty-first-century ballpark—cigarettes, fedoras, and typewriters.

My mind was racing as I made my way through the left-field bleachers. I was rattled after what Durocher and his boys had done to me. The eyepiece to the telescope was still in my front pocket. I patted my back pocket to make sure I had my pack of new baseball cards.

It would be simple to just go home at this point, I figured. I could find a quiet spot in a bathroom or something, do my thing with one of the cards in my pocket, and that would be the end of it. I'd certainly had enough excitement to last me a while.

But I didn't *want* to go home yet. I must admit, I was anxious to see if I had really changed history by stealing the eyepiece from the telescope. Maybe I could buy one of those bags of peanuts. Enjoy the game.

The ballplayers were warming up on the field, and I was kicking myself again for not bringing the little video camera my grandmother had given me for my birthday. It would have been so cool to shoot some footage of the players in 1951 and bring it back with me to show at home. Maybe I could have even made some money selling it to a collector. My dad would have liked that.

I thought about the butterfly effect. Maybe I had *already* changed history. If the Giants didn't replace the eyepiece of the telescope, they wouldn't be able to steal the catcher's signals. The game would be completely different. Bobby Thomson wouldn't hit the walk-off home run and be the hero. Ralph Branca wouldn't be the goat. Those two people in the stands who had heart attacks at the end of the game would continue to live.

And what about Willie Mays? If Thomson doesn't hit the homer, I thought, Willie could come to bat with the game on the line. Who knows what he might do?

It occurred to me that just *telling* Willie he would be on deck when the game ended could have changed things. Maybe now he would relax at the plate and get a hit earlier in the game to drive in some runs. Then, of course, the score would be different in the ninth inning and there would probably be no confrontation between Thomson and Branca.

There were so many variables to consider. If you change one little thing, it may very well change everything that happens after that—the butterfly effect.

But then I remembered there was another possibility I had to think about. What if Durocher had an extra eyepiece for the telescope in his desk drawer? He could simply screw it on, and the game would happen exactly as it would have before I showed up. The Giants would steal the signs and win the pennant by cheating.

Right or wrong, I came to a decision. I would at least try to let the Dodgers know their signs were being stolen. It might not make a difference one way or another, but in my gut it felt like the right thing to do.

There were a couple of policemen standing in front of the Dodger dugout, so I couldn't get in there to talk to anybody. I looked around. The bullpens were in fair territory, right next to the foul lines. I made my way over to the Dodger pen.

Some kids were hanging over the railing there, holding out scorecards and papers for players to autograph. I pushed my way through until I was able to get close to the rail.

There were only two Dodgers in the bullpen, casually tossing a ball back and forth. I recognized the one facing my direction—it was Ralph Branca! He looked a little younger than he had in my room the other night. If *anybody* needed to know his signs were being stolen, it was Branca. The guy he was playing catch with was closer to me, but his back was turned. His number was 29, but I didn't know who he was.

"Please, Ralph?" begged the kid next to me at the rail. "Gimme your autograph, *please*? I've been waiting all season."

Branca ignored the kid, but the other player turned around. He looked at the kids lining the railing, and suddenly made eye contact with me. His eyebrows went up.

"Stosh!" he yelled.

What? How did he know my name?

"You know that kid?" asked Branca.

"Sure I do!" the guy said, coming over to me at the railing. "You don't recognize me, do you?"

I looked at his face carefully. He was in his late twenties, I figured. Dark hair. Crew cut. But just about *all* the ballplayers looked like that in those days. I swore I had never seen that man in my life.

"It's *me*," he said, almost in a whisper as he put his big arms on my shoulders. "It's me, Flip."

Flip Valentini, my coach!

Of course! I had taken Flip back in time with me on a previous trip, and he was still there!

Here's what happened that day. Flip had been wishing he was young again, and when we arrived in 1942, he was eighteen years old. Flip and I had brought a radar gun with us because we wanted to see if Satchel Paige could throw a baseball a hundred miles an hour. That's when Flip fell in love with Laverne. As it turned out, Laverne's dad went nuts and tried to kill the both of us. I was forced to leave Flip back in 1942, where he married Laverne, learned how to throw the hesitation pitch from Satch, and got signed by the Dodgers. And now he was in the Polo Grounds at the same time as I was!

Flip lifted me out of the stands and gave me a big hug. It was great to see him, and he seemed *thrilled* to see me.

"You came back, Stosh!" he whispered. "I knew you would!"

He couldn't stop hugging me. Ralph Branca threw up his hands and went to find somebody else to warm him up.

I pulled Flip aside so the kids at the railing couldn't hear what I had to say.

"Flip, I have something really important I need to tell you," I whispered.

"Is it about the game today?"

"Yeah," I said. "The Giants—"

"I know. I *know*," Flip said. "Thomson's gonna hit a homer in the ninth to win it all. The Shot Heard Round the World."

"How do *you* know?" I asked.

"Because I already lived through it once, remember?" he said. "I lived through it when it first happened, and then you took me back in time with you, so I'm gonna have to live through it *again*."

I did the math in my head. I had left Flip in 1942. Now it was 1951. So he had been living in the past for nine years. *That's* why I didn't recognize him. He was nine years older.

"Stosh, I've been waiting a *long* time for you to come back," he said seriously. "Every time I see a kid your age out in the stands, I think it might be you, comin' back to get me."

"*Get* you?" I asked.

"Listen," Flip whispered in my ear, "you gotta get me outta here."

"Wh-why?" I asked, flustered. *This* I wasn't expecting.

"I can't take it," Flip said.

"But you're living everybody's dream, Flip!" I told him. "You're young again. You're pitching in the big leagues. You've got Laverne. You have your whole life ahead of you. Flip, you're going to be in the Baseball Hall of Fame, y'know. You got a second chance. You got to live your life over again."

"I know. I *know*," he said, shaking his head.

"So why would you want to give that up?"

"The problem is, I know *everything*," Flip told me. "I know who's gonna win this game, and exactly how. I know how the rest of my life is gonna play out. I know who's going to win the next dozen presidential elections. I know we're gonna have a war in Vietnam and we're gonna put a man on the moon. Nothing surprises me, Stosh! I pick up the newspaper and I know what's gonna be in it. So I put it down again. What's the point of reading it? Can you imagine what it's like to know everything that's going to happen before it happens?"

"I would think it would be cool," I admitted. "I would like that. You don't have to worry about anything."

"It's not cool, Stosh," he said. "I have to worry about *everything*. I have to be careful every day of my life. I'm afraid to do anything, touch anything, say anything, because I might change history, for the worse. It's like I'm walking around on eggshells all the time."

"The butterfly effect," I said. "That's what they call it. If a butterfly flaps its wings in Ohio, for instance . . ."

"I know, I *know*," Flip said wearily. "It could cause

a tornado in Hawaii. That's why I'm terrified that I might do something stupid and . . . I don't know, start World War III, or whatever. I vowed to myself that I wouldn't tamper with history, but it's not easy. It's a horrible way to live your life."

"Wow, I had no idea."

"I've given this a lotta thought, Stosh," Flip said. "And I decided that if you ever came back, I was gonna leave with you. I don't need to be in the Baseball Hall of Fame. I want my old life back. I want to experience *uncertainty* again. Bring me home with you, Stosh. I can't take it here anymore."

"What about Laverne?" I asked. "If you come home with me, she'll still be here. You'd show up in the twenty-first century, and she wouldn't be in your house. She wouldn't be your wife. It would be like you'd never met her."

"I would find her," Flip said. "I would track her down."

"And what if she married some other guy?" I asked.

"Laverne and I were made for each other," Flip said. "I'm sure she would choose me over some other guy."

Flip was talking crazy. Those nine years living in the past had done something to him.

"In my time, you're an old man, you know," I told him.

"I realize that," Flip said. "But I'd rather be an old man who doesn't know what's going to happen tomorrow than a young man who can predict the future."

He had completely blown my mind. I always thought that getting the chance to live your life over again would be the coolest thing *ever*. You could correct all the dumb mistakes you made the first time around. You could take advantage of opportunities you missed. But Flip had the chance to live his life all over again, and he hated it. He looked at me imploringly.

"I can take you with me, Flip," I said. "But there's something that I need to tell you."

"What?"

"Back home, in the twenty-first century, you had an accident," I told him, putting my hand on his shoulder. "You broke your hip falling in the dugout at one of my games."

"That I *didn't* know," he said. "Am I gonna be okay?"

"I don't know," I said. "The last time I saw you, you were in the hospital. The doctor told me you might not walk again."

"Is that all he said?" Flip asked.

"No," I told him honestly. "Flip, if I take you back home with me, we might get there and find you're dead."

12

A Good Day

WELL, *THAT* STOPPED FLIP COLD. THE THOUGHT OF TRAVEL-ing more than sixty years through time and finding himself dead on arrival definitely threw him for a loop.

"How could that even happen?" Flip asked. "Is that really possible?"

"I'm not sure," I admitted. "All I know is, when I was visiting you at the hospital, Laverne told me that mortality rates after hip fractures are really high for old guys."

Flip's forehead got all wrinkly. He was mulling it over.

"That may change stuff," he said. "What's the point of going home and havin' *that* happen to me? Livin' here like this has gotta be better than goin' home to Louisville to die. I gotta rethink this."

The game would be starting soon. The bleachers

were just about full now. Behind Flip, I could see
Ralph Branca throwing a ball back and forth with
one of his teammates. There were a few other Dodgers in the bullpen now, too. I had to keep my voice low.

"Flip, there's something else I need to tell you."

"Believe me, Stosh, anything you could possibly tell me about the game today, I know already.
Remember, I lived through this once. I know what's
gonna happen."

"Did you know that the Giants cheated?" I asked
him.

"Whaddaya mean they cheated?" Flip said. "You
mean they're gonna throw spitters or cork their
bats? Somethin' like that? Everybody does that stuff,
Stosh."

"No," I told him. "Well, they may be doing that
stuff, too. But they're stealing signs."

Flip laughed. "*Everybody* steals signs, Stosh! It's
part of the game. I told you that a million times."

"Not like that," I told him. I pointed to center
field. "See that window? That's Leo Durocher's office.
He's got a telescope up there."

"So?"

"It's pointing at home plate," I told Flip, "and
right next to the telescope on the desk is a buzzer
system. When you push the button, it buzzes down in
the Giants bullpen. You see? They steal the catcher's
signs and tip off their batters what the next pitch is
going to be."

"Are you *kidding* me?" Flip asked, raising his

voice almost a little too loud. "Jeez, how do you know all this, Stosh?"

"I saw it with my own eyes," I said. "I was up there."

"I-I can't believe it. I mean, I know Durocher likes to win and all, but . . ."

I took the eyepiece out of my pocket and handed it to Flip.

"Look," I said. "I took this off the telescope. But for all I know, Durocher has another one."

"Holy moly!" Flip replied, slapping his forehead. "I had no idea. This changes everything."

I didn't bother telling Flip that Durocher and his boys had roughed me up and tied me up in the equipment room, or that Willie Mays had rescued me. He had enough information to process.

Flip was clearly floored by what I had told him, and furious, too. After it had sunk in, he looked over at the Giants' dugout, where Leo Durocher was talking with his players.

"Cheaters!" Flip said, spitting on the ground. "We had a thirteen-game lead on those guys! Now I know how they won all those games at the end of the season and caught up with us. And people call *us* bums."

"And it goes into the record books for all time that the Giants won the pennant," I said.

Flip had calmed down a little. Now, I could tell, he was plotting strategy.

"So in the ninth inning, Thomson's gonna know what pitch is coming," he said. "If they can't steal our signs, he won't hit the Shot Heard Round the World and they won't win the pennant."

"Probably not," I agreed.

"And Ralph won't be the biggest goat in baseball history for the rest of his life," Flip added.

"Right."

"Ralph is one of my best friends on this team," Flip said. "I can't let the Giants ruin his life. I've gotta do something."

"I thought you made a vow not to change history," I said to Flip. "Aren't you worried about the butterfly effect?"

"Yeah, but I'm worried about Ralph, too. This is just wrong. I can do something to make it right. Lemme think."

I figured Flip was going to suggest we tamper with Thomson's bat or throw a pitch at his head to knock him out of the game. But he had a different plan.

"Here's what I'm gonna do," he whispered. "In the ninth inning, when it's time for Ralph to come into the game and pitch to Thomson, I'm gonna convince Dressen to bring *me* in instead."

"What?" I exclaimed. "But then *you'll* be the goat for the rest of your life!"

"That's not gonna happen, Stosh. If the catcher calls for a fastball, I'll throw my curve. If he calls for the curve, I'll throw my fastball. If the Giants steal our signs, they'll be stealing the wrong signs. And if Thomson is expecting my fastball and I throw him the curve, no way is he gonna hit it. I'll probably strike him out on three pitches. I'll be the hero."

"What if Thomson hits a homer off you fair and square?" I asked Flip. "Then you're the goat."

"I'm willing to take that chance," Flip replied. "Listen, Stosh. I've lived my life. Twice now. Whatever happens to me, good or bad, I can handle it. But I don't want this to happen to Ralph."

A marching band came out on the field to play the national anthem. Flip told me he was going to run over to talk with manager Charlie Dressen and plant the idea in his head to bring *him* in during the late innings.

"Don't move, Stosh," Flip instructed me, as he turned to run to the dugout. "I'll be right—"

What happened next is painful to describe. Somebody had left a couple of bats on the ground next to the bullpen. As Flip turned to take his first step, his right cleat landed on the thick end of one of the bats and he went sprawling. He tried to avoid it, but his left foot landed on the other bat. There was a sickening crack when he hit the ground.

Oh no, not *again*!

"Owwww!" Flip hollered. "Who left these damn bats here?"

Flip was moaning in pain. A bunch of the Dodgers came running over. I recognized Jackie Robinson and a few of the others. They all gathered around Flip, who was writhing on the dirt.

"Somebody get a doctor," Ralph Branca shouted.

The national anthem was delayed. An umpire came running over to see what was going on. So did the Dodgers' trainer. He sliced open the leg of Flip's uniform with a pair of scissors and touched the skin on Flip's left leg. Flip yelled in pain.

"I think it's broken," he said, grimacing.

"We need to get you to the hospital so they can set this," said the trainer.

A few of the Dodgers groaned. Baseball players tend to be superstitious. This could not be a good omen.

Ralph Branca and Jackie Robinson helped Flip get to his feet and hobble gingerly off the field. I opened the door for them so they could bring Flip into the clubhouse while he waited for the ambulance to arrive. They put him down on one of those training tables they use for massages.

"Joe Stoshack!" Jackie said, noticing who I was for the first time. "I haven't seen you in years, Stosh!"

Jackie gave me a hug and told me it was good to see me again. Once again, I did the math in my head. I had visited him in 1947. To him, it was four years ago.

"Kid, you're pretty popular around here," Branca told me.

"We better go," Jackie said. "The game is gonna start any minute."

"Wait!" Flip said, grabbing Jackie's sleeve. "Stosh and I have to tell you guys something. Tell 'em, Stosh."

I wish Flip had done the talking, but he was in a lot of pain and clearly wanted me to do it. So I did. I told Jackie and Ralph exactly what was going to happen in the ninth inning. The score would be 4–2. Ralph would be brought in to face Bobby Thomson. He would slam Ralph's second pitch into the left field stands to win the game and the pennant.

They listened to me carefully, their eyes getting wider with every word I said.

"That's crazy," Ralph said. "Are you *sure?*"

"The kid knows," Flip said. "He's from the future."

"Durocher is stealing your signs," I told Ralph. "He's got a telescope in his office in center field."

"Why, that dirty rat!" Branca said. "I should go over there and—"

"Fuhgetaboutit," Flip said. "All you gotta do is ignore the catcher's signs and throw a different pitch to Thomson. That'll throw him off stride."

"It sounds crazy," Jackie said.

"I know," said Flip. "But it's gonna work."

"Okay, if you say so."

"Trust us, Ralph," Flip assured him.

Ralph and Jackie said good-bye and ran back out on the field. Flip lay back on the training table, still grimacing in pain but also breathing a sigh of relief.

"We *did* it, Stosh," he told me. "If Ralph does what we told him to do, everything's gonna be different when you get back home to Louisville. The record books will say that we won the pennant. There'll be no Shot Heard Round the World."

I heard the national anthem playing out on the field.

"The ambulance will be here soon," I told Flip. "Is it okay with you if I go watch the game?"

"Sure, Stosh," he said. "You go have fun. Get yourself a bag of peanuts or somethin'."

". . . for the land of the free . . . and the home . . . of the . . . brave."

The crowd let out a cheer and I heard the umpire shout, "Play ball!"

I was about to open the door when somebody pounded on it from the other side.

"Who's in there?" a gruff voice shouted.

I backed away from the door, almost falling down. The Giants! They must have found out that I escaped from the supply room and they were looking for me. I signaled to Flip to let him know I wasn't supposed to be there.

"Me!" Flip shouted. "Flip Valentini."

"Is there a kid in there?" the voice shouted. "About thirteen years old? I heard somebody."

"No!" Flip shouted back. "Just me."

"Open the door!" the voice shouted. "This is the police!"

"I gotta get outta here!" I whispered in Flip's ear. "Is there another door?"

"No! Why are the cops chasing you?"

"No time to explain," I whispered. "I'm going to go home. Are you sure you don't want to come with me?"

"Nah," Flip replied. "My broken leg is gonna heal.

But I don't wanna get home and find I'm dead. You get outta here."

"Open the door or I'll bust it down!" the voice on the other side shouted.

"I'll be right there!" Flip hollered. "I hurt my leg. I gotta hop."

Flip motioned for me to hurry up. I pulled the pack of new cards out of my pocket and ripped the wrapper off. I took one of the cards at random. It didn't matter who was on it. The card would take me back to the present day.

"Good luck, Flip," I told him as I pulled up a folding chair and sat down.

"You too," Flip replied. "Don't you worry about me. I'll be fine."

There wasn't a lot of confidence in his voice. I knew Flip was suffering going through his life again in the past. But I also knew he was going to suffer in the future. There was nothing I could do about it.

"I'll give you ten seconds," the voice shouted. "Then I come in there."

It didn't take long. I began to feel the tingling sensation in the tips of my fingers. It was like the purring of a cat, almost. Buzzy. It was a pleasant feeling.

"Ten! Nine! Eight!" the voice shouted.

I thought about what I had accomplished. I had busted up Leo Durocher's little cheating system and told the Dodgers about it. The Giants could still possibly win the game and the pennant, but they would have to win it fair and square. I had done the right thing. And I had even met the great Willie Mays. The Branca card had been destroyed, but all in all it was a good day. The tingling sensation was getting stronger. I could feel it all over my hand, and it gradually crept up my wrist, arm, and shoulder. I thought about what it would be like to go home.

"Seven! Six! Five! Four!"

The feeling swept across my body. Everything was vibrating now. I had reached the point of no return. It wouldn't be long.

"Three! Two! One! Okay, I'm breakin' down the door!"

That was the last thing I heard, except for a whooshing noise. Then I was gone.

13

Unintended Consequences

"WATCH OUT!" MY MOTHER SCREAMED AS I CAME SAILING across the living room.

My foot hit the little step at the edge of the door-way and I tripped. I dodged the wing chair and swerved around the bookcase, but fell on the cof-fee table, landed on the wood floor with a thud, and almost rolled into the fireplace.

"Ooof!"

"Were you in the past, Joey?" my mom asked as she rushed to my side to check for bumps and bruises. "What happened? Are you okay?"

"Yeah. Can't talk now, Mom," I said hurriedly as I got up to brush the ashes off my pants. "It's a long story! I'll be right back to tell you all about it."

With that, I rushed upstairs to my bedroom and turned on my computer. It's an old machine, but I use it only for writing school papers and looking stuff up online. It took forever to boot up, but finally I was able to get on Google.

I typed "Shot Heard Round the World." That ought to do it.

There were *millions* of results. That didn't surprise me, or bother me. You type just about *anything* into Google and you get millions of results.

The first one that came up was the Wikipedia entry about the gunshot in Concord, Massachusetts, that supposedly touched off the Revolutionary War in 1775. Then there was this poem about it by Ralph Waldo Emerson. . . .

By the rude bridge that arched the flood,
Their flag to April's breeze unfurled,
Here once the embattled farmers stood,
And fired the shot heard round the world.

The next entry was about the 1914 assassination of Archduke Franz Ferdinand of Austria. That was the spark that started World War I, and it was *also* called "The Shot Heard Round the World." I had never heard of that one.

I scrolled down. Apparently, *whenever* something really amazing happens, somebody calls it "The Shot Heard Round the World." When Vice President Dick Cheney accidentally shot his friend on a hunting trip, it was called "The Shot Heard Round the World." There were golf shots heard round the world. Basketball shots heard round the world. Hockey shots heard round the world.

But nothing about baseball. I kept scrolling down the list. There was nothing about Bobby Thomson. Nothing about Ralph Branca.

A smile crept across my face. It was like it had never happened! The history books were wiped clean!

"It never happened!" I heard myself shouting gleefully.

"What never happened?" my mom called from downstairs. "Is everything okay, Joey?"

I couldn't believe it! It never happened!

I wasn't going to start crowing about my success until I was sure. Maybe I had made a mistake.

I clicked away from Google and checked to see the final standings for the National League in 1951. . . .

Brooklyn Dodgers: *98–59*
New York Giants: *97–60*
St. Louis Cardinals: 81–73
Boston Braves: *76–78*

That was the *proof*! The Dodgers won the pennant! History had been changed, and it was all because of *me*.

"I *did* it!" I shouted.

"Did *what*?" my mother called from downstairs. "Come down and tell us what's going on, Joey."

For once in my life, I had done exactly what I set out to do. I had traveled back in time and changed the historical record, just as I had intended.

I pulled *The Baseball Encyclopedia* off my bookshelf and flipped to the section where it says who won the pennant every year. It said the same thing that I read online. The Dodgers won the 1951 pennant.

Even *paperbound* books had been changed! How could that be? It didn't matter. I didn't care. It happened. That's all that counted. And it was because of *me*.

What a rush! I felt such a feeling of euphoria, a feeling of power. I ran downstairs to tell my mom and Uncle Wilbur the good news.

"I did it!" I shouted even before I got to the first floor. "I changed history! I am all-powerful! Bow down before me!"

"Calm down," my mother said. "How did you change history, Joey?"

"I wiped Bobby Thomson's Shot Heard Round the World right out of the record books!" I boasted. "Now it's like it never happened."

"Bobby who?" Mom asked. "What are you talking about?"

"See!" I said. "That proves it! You don't even know about it anymore. But you knew about it yesterday, before I left."

"You're talking crazy, Joey," my mother said.

"The boy is loco," said Uncle Wilbur.

"You need something to eat," my mom told me. "Come on, wash your hands. I'm about to put food on the table."

I stopped. *Wait a minute.* A thought had crossed

my mind. If Thomson didn't hit the Shot Heard Round the World, and Branca didn't throw the pitch that became the Shot Heard Round the World . . .

"How did the game end?" I asked.

"Beats me," said my mother. "I don't even know what game you're talking about. Come eat."

I looked to Uncle Wilbur. He wasn't a diehard baseball fanatic, but he followed the game. Surely he would know what happened. He'd been a young man back then.

"Do you know what happened in the last game of 1951?" I asked him.

"How should I know?" Uncle Wilbur told me. "That was over sixty years ago. It was just another game."

"But you've heard of Ralph Branca and Bobby Thomson, haven't you?" I asked.

"Nope," he replied.

"What about Willie Mays?" I asked.

"Willie who?" said my mother.

"Wait. What?" I asked. "You mean to say you've never heard of Willie Mays?"

"Wasn't he that guy who used to make infomercials for OxiClean or something?" asked my mom.

"That was *Billy* Mays!" I shouted. "Willie Mays is one of the most famous baseball players in history! How could you not know that name? Even people who don't follow baseball know about Willie Mays."

"Never heard of the guy," said Uncle Wilbur.

I couldn't believe it.

"Wait a minute, are you putting me on?" I asked, looking back and forth between the two of them. My mother has been known to play pranks on me from time to time, but my uncle does not joke.

"Are you feeling all right, Joey?" my mother asked. "Maybe you have a temperature."

Maybe I did. I felt myself sweating. She put her hand on my forehead.

"I'll be right back," I said. Then I dashed back upstairs.

"What happened to Willie Mays?" I mumbled to myself as I typed his name on my keyboard.

Willie Robertson. Willie Nelson. Willie Geist. Willie McBrides . . .

There was no Wikipedia entry for Willie Mays! How could that be?

I checked the website for the National Baseball Hall of Fame.

No Willie Mays! He wasn't in the Hall of Fame anymore!

Frantically, I looked up Willie Mays in *The Baseball Encyclopedia*. Ah, there he was. . . .

Year	Team	Games	At bats	Hits	Doubles	Triples	Homers	Runs	RBI	Walks	Steals	Avg.
1951	Giants	121	464	127	22	5	20	59	68	56	7	.274

What? Willie Mays only played that one season! Just 1951. That was *it*. Nothing after that. It was like he vanished off the face of the earth.

Oh no! What happened to Willie Mays?

Something was horribly wrong. I knew that Mays played all through the fifties, sixties, and even into the seventies, when he was over forty years old.

What did I do?

I was frantic now. I searched around online until I found the play-by-play for that final playoff game of 1951 to see what happened. It was all the same into the ninth inning. . . .

Dark singles. Mueller singles. Dark to third.
Irvin fouls out. One out. Lockman doubles.
4–2. Runners on second and third. Thomson
up. Branca comes in. Ball one.

And that's when history changed.

Instead of hitting the Shot Heard Round the World on the second pitch, Thomson took it for ball two. Then he took ball three. Then he took ball four.

It said Thomson walked on four pitches! That loaded the bases and brought Willie Mays to the plate.

Oh man! I told Willie he was going to be in the on-deck circle when the game ended. He must have freaked out when Thomson drew a walk. Willie had told me that he didn't want to come to the plate with the game on the line. And because I told the Dodgers that the Giants were stealing their signs, that's exactly what happened.

A single by Willie would have tied up the game. An extra base hit would have won it. Even if Willie had struck out or popped up, it wouldn't have been a disaster because there was only one out when he came to the plate. The next batter would have had a shot to win the game.

Then I read what happened. . . .

The 21-year-old rookie Willie Howard Mays, playing in the game of his life and clearly under tremendous pressure, hit into a weak double play to end the game, and the season.

Oh no!

If Willie didn't play in the major leagues after 1951, that meant the season-ending double play was his last major league at bat. His final swing.

But why didn't he play the next year?

I did a little more digging online. I found a 1951 article in a newspaper from Westfield, Alabama, where Willie Mays was born in 1931. It said that he came home at the end of the season and decided to take a break from baseball. There were a few other articles in the same newspaper. They said that Willie Mays, "formerly a player on the New York Giants," had taken a job working "in a laundry."

Oh no. Willie must have been devastated about what happened at the end of the 1951 season. He never returned to baseball. He never became a star. He was a nobody.

And it was my fault.

It got worse.

Local man William Howard Mays passed
away on Wednesday at his home in Westfield.
A laundry worker for nineteen years, Mays
played one season for the New York Giants as
a young man.

The obituary was dated 1970. He never even made it to his fortieth birthday.

I started crying and cursing.

This was a *disaster*! Willie Mays had rescued me when I was tied up in the equipment closet, and how had I repaid him? I had ruined his life!

"Are you okay, Joey?" my mother asked. She had come upstairs and was standing at my bedroom door.

"I did a terrible thing, Mom. I made a big mistake."

She came in and put her arm around me.

"Oh, whatever it is, I'm sure it couldn't be that bad," she told me.

"It's bad, Mom!" I insisted. "I ruined Willie Mays's life."

"Shhh, it's okay, Joey," my mother said, stroking my forehead. "Nobody ever heard of that guy."

"Nobody ever heard of him because I ruined his life!" I told her. "I gotta fix it. I have to make it right."

14

A New Mission

AS I RAN UPSTAIRS TO MY ROOM, MY MIND WAS RACING
again. By telling the Dodgers that the Giants were
stealing their signs, I had dramatically altered the
lives of at least three players: Ralph Branca, Bobby
Thomson, and Willie Mays. I had taken away their
fame. I had robbed them of the money they would
have earned from that fame. I had turned all three of
them into nobodies. And who knew what *other* problems I might have caused?

I needed to fix things. But how? If only life had
an undo button we could press and erase the latest
dumb mistake we made.

One thing was for sure—I had to go back to 1951
again.

I grabbed the plaque my dad had given me for my
birthday. The Branca card was gone, of course. That
jerk Leo Durocher had ripped it up right in front

of my face. I grabbed a razor blade and carefully separated the Bobby Thomson card from the wood. Things had to go right this time. This was the only 1951 card I had left.

I climbed onto my bed and got ready for the trip. Before I had even picked up the card, there was a knock on the door. It was my mom and Uncle Wilbur.

"Here, I made you a sandwich," my mother said, handing me a paper bag.

"I don't want a sandwich!" I barked at her. "That's not important! I gotta go save Willie Mays!"

"What are you wasting your time on *that* guy for?" Uncle Wilbur asked. "He was a nobody."

"Can you close the door, *please?*"

"You be careful, Joey," my mother said, almost pleading.

"I will. I *will*," I said. "Just close the door. I'll be back as soon as I can. I promise."

They closed the door. I knew my mother was still standing there, listening, but I didn't care. There were more important things to worry about.

I took a deep breath. I *would* need to be careful, I thought before picking up the Bobby Thomson card. This was no time to do something rash. It would just get me into trouble again later. I didn't want to ruin anybody *else's* life.

Think. *Think. What am I going to do when I get to 1951? What can I do to change things back to the way they were?*

I looked around my bedroom. My eyes fell upon

the small box at the edge of my desk. The little video camera that my grandmother had given me for my birthday was in there.

Of course!

I opened the box and slipped the little camera in my pocket. Then I picked up the Bobby Thomson card. It was my ticket to 1951. I closed my eyes and tried to get in the mood. It wasn't easy. I had a lot on my mind. This was going to be a mission that I *had* to complete. I couldn't mess up this time. If I failed, Willie Mays would be a failure. And I would never be able to forgive myself.

It took a while—longer than usual. There were no tingles in my fingertips. No nothing.

I was getting impatient. Maybe I had damaged the Thomson card when I cut it off the plaque. Maybe I had lost my power to travel through time. I had always worried that as I grew older, one day my power would be gone—like when a boy's voice changes around my age.

Maybe I was just pressing, like a batter who's trying too hard to get a hit, and he can't hit *anything*. Or maybe I was only able to travel back to the same year once. Who knows what could have gone wrong?

But then, when I was just about to give up, something happened. I started to feel that old familiar tingling sensation in the tips of my fingers.

It was happening, and it happened fast this time. I was buzzing all over. I felt lightheaded and dizzy. I really should have had something to eat. But no time for that. Atom by atom, my body was deconstructing in the present day and reassembling itself in the past. It was the strangest feeling.

"Joey, is everything okay in there?" my mother asked.

And then I felt myself vanish.

15

Like Magic

THIS TIME—FOR A CHANGE—I LANDED EXACTLY WHERE I wanted to be and when I wanted to be there. I was right outside the Polo Grounds. *Perfect.* It was early in the day, just as I'd hoped. The place looked deserted. I ran over to the same chain-link fence I'd scaled the first time, and dug a toe into it. So far, so good.

"Hey, you!" somebody yelled.

Uh-oh.

I stopped and turned around slowly.

There was a cop standing there. Or maybe he was a security guard. He was wearing a uniform, but he didn't have a gun on his belt. Just some kind of a billy club. His arms were folded across his chest.

"Whaddaya think you doin' here?" he asked gruffly.

"Nothing."

"It's Wednesday. Why ain't you in school?" he said.

"I . . . I . . ." I had nothing to say.

"Don't you know that trespassin' is against the law?" the guy said. "I should turn you in."

Oh no. Not again. This could not be a good thing.

On second thought, maybe it *could* be a good thing. I hopped down off the fence and stuck out my hand like he and I were old friends. He didn't shake it.

"I need to talk to Leo Durocher," I said, trying to sound confident. "It's very important. A matter of life and death, really."

The guy looked at me for a long time, as if he was trying to figure me out. He fingered his billy club, like he was looking for a reason to use it. I wasn't about to make any sudden moves.

"Talk to Mr. Durocher about *what*?" he asked.

"I have something that he needs," I said.

I didn't want to tell this security guard any more than he needed to know.

"Mr. Durocher ain't here yet," he said. "The game don't start for hours. If you have somethin' to give 'im, give it to me and I'll pass it along."

I wasn't sure if I could trust the guy. But I didn't have a whole lot of choices. Maybe I could try dazzling him, I figured. I pulled my little video camera out of my pocket.

"What's that?" he asked.

"It's a camera."

"That ain't no camera," he replied, laughing. "That thing's too little to be a camera. There's no place to put the film."

"It doesn't use film," I said, pushing the power button. "Look."

The screen lit up. I pointed the camera across the street from the ballpark, so he could see the view with his own eyes and also see it on the screen at the same time.

The security guard's mouth dropped open.

I knew that digital cameras came along sometime in the 1980s. Before then, cameras recorded their images on film, not computer chips. One time, my uncle Wilbur showed me an old film camera that he keeps on his bookshelf. With film, you didn't see what you were shooting on a screen—you looked through what they called a "viewfinder." It was just a little window in the camera.

You couldn't see your picture instantly, either. You had to send the film out to a lab to be "developed." And you couldn't shoot movies with a regular camera in those days. You had to have two separate devices to shoot movies and still pictures. This security guy had never seen anything like my camera.

I shot a selfie with him in it, and then held the camera up so he could see the picture on the screen.

"Holy smokes!" he exclaimed. "Where'd you get that thing?"

"It was a present from my grandmother," I said honestly. "Watch this. It's called *zoom*."

I pushed the button that enlarges the image. His jaw dropped open again as he watched the picture of himself get bigger and bigger until the screen was filled with just his eyes and nose.

It was like I had dangled shiny beads in front of a tribe of primitive people. The guy no longer had any interest in hitting me with his club or turning me in. His eyes were wide.

"Is that magic?" he asked.

"No, it's digital," I replied, knowing he wouldn't understand. "Look, I need you to do something very important. I need you to give this camera to Leo Durocher."

"Why?"

"He'll know what to do with it," I said. "But it's *really* important that you show him how to do the zoom thing with this button. Can you do that for me?"

"Yeah, I guess so. Okay."

To make sure he understood, I showed him how to turn the camera on and use the zoom button again.

It was a long shot, I knew. But I had a hunch that as soon as Leo Durocher saw what my camera could do, the first thing he would think of was how he could use it to cheat. And zooming in with my video camera would serve the exact same purpose as using a telescope to steal signs. I felt bad about giving away the camera my grandmother had given me as a present, but this was a matter of life and death.

"Thank you," I said to the security guard.

There was no reason for me to stick around. I ran across the street and ducked into an alley between two buildings. I pulled out a new baseball card, sat down on the ground, and closed my eyes.

Home, I thought. *I just want to go home and stay there. I will never do this again. It's too risky.*

It didn't take long for the tingling sensation to come and take me away. This time, I didn't go flying across the living room. I went flying across the kitchen. Narrowly missing the kitchen table, I swerved to avoid going headfirst into the refrigerator, and almost knocked the little TV off its stand.

Uncle Wilbur was sitting there. Mom was standing at the stove.

"You're just in time," she said, almost matter-of-factly. She was getting used to my comings and goings. "We're having chicken."

"Did you guys ever hear of Willie Mays?" I asked as I was getting up.

"Of *course* we've heard of Willie Mays," my mother said. "Why?"

"I *told* you the boy is loco," said Uncle Wilbur.

"Are you feeling okay, Joey?" my mother asked as she put her hand on my forehead.

I wasn't convinced.

"Who *was* he?" I asked. "Who was Willie Mays?"

"He was a baseball player," my mother replied. "Everybody knows that."

"He played for the Giants," added Uncle Wilbur. "Superstar. One of the best ever."

I had to be sure. I ran upstairs and woke up my computer. It didn't take a lot of searching online to confirm that everything checked out. The Giants won the 1951 pennant. Thomson hit the Shot Heard Round the World, and was the hero. Branca was the goat. Willie Mays was on deck when the game ended, and he went on to a long, successful Hall of Fame career. There is even a large statue of him in front of the ballpark where the Giants play today.

"Yes!"

The security guard *did* give my camera to Leo Durocher! The Giants used it to steal the signs. It had worked like a charm. History had been changed back again.

I let out a tremendous sigh of relief. I had messed things up terribly, but I was able to go back and fix them. A feeling of happiness . . . giddiness . . . came over me. I came running down the stairs.

"I did it!" I announced. "I, Joe Stoshack, single-handedly saved Willie Mays's life!"

"Good," said my mom. "Come eat. It's getting cold."

"The boy is loco," said Uncle Wilbur.

While we were eating, my mom's cell phone rang. She doesn't like to take calls during dinner, but every so often there's an emergency so she always checks to see who's calling. She took the phone into the living room and had a short, whispered conversation with somebody.

"That was Laverne Valentini," she said when she came back. "Flip isn't doing well. We'd better get over to the hospital."

I grabbed a piece of chicken and ran out the door.

16

Another Birthday Present

ON THE WAY TO THE HOSPITAL, MY MOTHER WAS DRIVING faster than she usually does. I hoped she wouldn't get pulled over by the police.

When we got to Flip's room, Laverne was sitting in a chair next to the bed, holding Flip's hand. His eyes were closed. The lights were dim. A doctor and nurse were looking at monitors that were hooked up to Flip. He had tubes running into his nose and an IV in his arm. At his bedside I noticed a book titled *Physics of the Impossible*.

"How is he?" my mother whispered.

"We're doing all we can for him," replied the doctor without looking up.

"He is what he is," said Laverne.

Flip seemed agitated. His eyes were closed, but he was gesturing with his hands.

"These physicists in Italy say they've seen subatomic neutrinos travelin' faster than the speed of light," Flip mumbled to nobody in particular. "So it's possible to go back in time. The flux capacitor can reverse the polarity of the wormhole."

"Shhh," Laverne leaned over to whisper in Flip's ear. "Everything's okay, honey."

Flip started ranting something about vacuum chambers, fiber optics, and semitransparent beam splitters. He wasn't making any sense.

"It's the drugs," the nurse told us. "They make him delirious."

"Think about it," Flip mumbled. "In just one second, a cheetah can run thirty-four yards. A telephone signal can travel 100,000 miles. A hummingbird can beat its wings seventy times. Eight million blood cells can die. . . ."

"Try to rest, Mr. Valentini," said the nurse.

I wanted to tell Flip about my adventure going back and forth to save Willie Mays, but it didn't seem like the right time or place.

Suddenly, Flip stopped ranting. He opened his eyes and looked up at me.

"Stosh . . ."

"Yeah, it's me, Flip," I said. I leaned over the bed and took his hand.

"We gotta get to the game, Stosh!" he said urgently. "We're gonna be late."

"There's no game, Flip," I told him. "Don't worry about that."

"No game?"

He looked up at me. His eyes were clear. I shook my head.

"No game," I said.

Flip nodded slightly and took a deep breath. Then he closed his eyes.

A second later, beeping noises came out of the monitors that were hooked up to Flip. The doctor and nurse started frantically pressing on Flip's chest, blowing air into his mouth, and giving him shots. A few more doctors came running in and started working on him.

"What's happening?" I asked.

"You folks need to leave," one of the doctors said. But we weren't going anywhere.

Flip wasn't responding. His chest wasn't moving up and down. He wasn't breathing. The monitors were still beeping. Laverne and my mom started crying.

After a few intense minutes, the first doctor stepped away from the bed and pulled off his rubber gloves.

"That's it," he said, looking at his watch and then at Laverne. "I'm sorry, ma'am. We did what we could."

I never really appreciated how famous Flip was until he died. His name was all over the news that night, and there were stories about him in the papers and online, too. Our phone rang off the hook.

Flip's funeral was held a few days later. I wore my nice jacket and tie and we went to this fancy funeral parlor on Taylorsville Road in Louisville. The place was filled with flowers. Hundreds of people had come from all over the country. Some of them were famous baseball players. Some of them were just fans. All the players on my team were there, of course. Some of their parents came, too. My dad showed up. Flip was so loved by so many people.

It was a really nice ceremony. Everybody was sniffling and sobbing and handing out tissues while they swapped stories about Flip. A bunch of people got up to talk. Before the funeral, Laverne had asked me if I wanted to say a few words. After all, I had played a pretty big part in Flip's life.

But what was I going to do—get up there and tell everybody that Flip and I traveled back in time together? I couldn't say that I left him in 1942, and that's when he met Laverne and learned how to throw the hesitation pitch from Satchel Paige. Nobody would believe it. They would think I was being disrespectful, or just plain crazy. I probably would have been thrown out of the funeral parlor.

It didn't matter. I wouldn't have been able to make it past the first sentence anyway. I'm not all that emotional, myself. But every time somebody said something about Flip, I would get this lump in my throat and I had to fight back tears.

When the funeral was over and people started to say their good-byes and head for their cars, Laverne put her arm around me and told me she wanted to speak with me privately. There were some dark, streaky lines on her face from the tears that had mixed with her makeup. I went with her to a little room behind the chapel.

"I wanted to thank you again, Stosh," she told me, holding my hand. "If it hadn't been for you, I never would have met Flip in the first place. I shudder to think what my life would have been like if he hadn't come into it. We had so many wonderful years together."

"You're welcome," I said awkwardly.

I didn't know what else to say. When somebody says "thank you," it seems like you should say "you're welcome." But it just sounded a little bit strange in this situation.

"Oh, one more thing," Laverne said, as she opened a closet door and pulled out a long, thin box that was wrapped in red paper. "This is for you. Think of it as another birthday present."

What could she possibly be giving me? The box was about the size of a skateboard. But why would Flip's wife be giving me a skateboard? I'd never expressed any interest in skateboarding.

"What is it?" I asked.

"Flip had been talking about liquidating the inventory of the store for a long time," Laverne told me. "So before he went into the hospital, he had this made. He told me he wanted you to have it."

I tore off the wrapping paper and opened the box. I was relieved that it wasn't a skateboard. It was a wooden plaque, very much like the one my father had given me for my birthday, but longer. Instead of two baseball cards mounted on it, there were ten.

Honus Wagner. Jackie Robinson. Babe Ruth. Shoeless Joe Jackson. Satchel Paige. Ray Chapman. Jim Thorpe. Roberto Clemente. Ted Williams. They were all in a line. And the last card on the right was Flip, in his Brooklyn Dodgers uniform.

That's when I lost it. During the funeral, I had come close to crying a few times, but I managed to hold it in. There was no stopping it now. I was blubbering like a baby. Laverne held me and we cried together.

17

Sometimes History Can Change You

THE PLAQUE WITH ALL THOSE BASEBALL CARDS ON IT WAS the nicest gift anyone had ever given to me. It was definitely worth a lot of money, and the smart thing to do would be to lock it up in a safe somewhere.

But that didn't seem right. I decided that I was going to put it up on the wall of my bedroom, right above my desk so I could look at it for inspiration while I was doing my homework and stuff. Maybe we could get an alarm system or something to prevent anyone from breaking into the house and stealing it.

The day after Flip's funeral, I decided for sure that it was time to announce my "retirement." I wasn't going to travel through time anymore.

It had been fun, and I'd had some amazing experiences. But I decided that going back in time was simply too dangerous. I had been kidnapped, shot at, attacked, and nearly killed on numerous occasions. If anything ever happened to me and I didn't make it back to the present day, I don't know if my mom could handle it.

And after what happened with Willie Mays, I finally realized how powerful the butterfly effect could be. It was way too easy for me to change some little thing in the past that would have a dramatic impact on the future.

At least now, I had this beautiful plaque so I could think back about the trips I had been on, and to remind me of Flip.

I remembered the time I had dinner with Babe Ruth in New York City. Man, that guy could *eat*. He got sick and threw up all over the place.

I remembered going fishing with Ted Williams, hunting with Satchel Paige, and meeting Lou Gehrig on a train to Chicago.

I remembered the batting lesson I got from the great Honus Wagner.

I remembered the time I went to bed wishing I could experience what Jackie Robinson experienced when he broke the color barrier. And when I woke up, I was an African-American kid in 1947.

Those were the good old days, for me. How lucky I was to have lived through them and met all those great players.

It would be cool to go back in time and visit those guys again. But no, I just couldn't risk it anymore.

The gift from Flip would have to do. That night, I fell asleep cradling the plaque in my arms.

It must have been around midnight when I heard something. We have an old house, and it creaks with the wind and cold. But this was a different sound. I opened my eyes.

Then I bolted upright. There wasn't a man in my room this time. No, this time there was a *crowd* of people standing around my bed.

I tried to scream, but no sound came out of my mouth. I hugged the plaque to my chest, as if it would protect me. They had me way outnumbered, and some of them were holding bats. What were they going to do to me?

"Shhhh," somebody whispered. "It's okay, Stosh."

It was dark, so I couldn't make them out at first. But after my eyes adjusted to the little night-light, I could see they were all wearing baseball uniforms. And then I was able to make out their faces.

Honus Wagner. Jackie Robinson. Babe Ruth. Shoeless Joe Jackson. Satchel Paige. Ray Chapman. Jim Thorpe. Roberto Clemente. Ted Williams.

All the guys on the plaque were there, including Flip. It was young Flip, and he was wearing his Brooklyn Dodgers uniform.

"W-what's going on?" I asked. "What are you all doing here?"

"You must have wished for it, Stosh," Flip told me, "and you made it happen. Just like all the other times."

"We came back," said Honus Wagner, coming over to shake my hand. "It's good to see you again, Stosh."

The others came over one by one to shake hands with me, too.

I couldn't *believe* it. I knew that I could take people back in time with me, because I'd done it with my dad, my mom, and Flip. And I knew that I could *pull* people from their time into my time, because I'd done it with Honus, Bobby Thomson, and Ralph Branca. But pulling *ten* people through time, simultaneously? Now, *that* was impressive.

I looked around the room at their faces. Ray Chapman and Roberto Clemente, two players from completely different eras, were standing next to each other. I remembered that both of them would die tragically, Clemente in a plane crash and Chapman getting his skull fractured by a pitched ball. That's why I had traveled back in time to meet them. I was trying to prevent Roberto from getting on that plane in 1972, and to prevent Ray from stepping into that batter's box in 1920. I had failed both times.

On the other side of my bed was Shoeless Joe Jackson. He had been kicked out of baseball for life because of a gambling scandal he hadn't even participated in. I had traveled back to 1919 trying to prevent it from happening. That hadn't worked out, either.

Now that I was looking at their faces, it occurred to me that I had *always* failed when I went back in time. I wasn't able to see whether or not Babe Ruth called his famous "called shot" home run in 1932. Ted Williams and I hadn't been able to warn President Roosevelt about the attack on Pearl Harbor. I hadn't been able to prevent the assassination of Abraham Lincoln in 1865.

I was a failure. Maybe that's why they were all in my bedroom now, I figured—to get back at me.

"I'm so sorry," I said to the group. "Every time I went back in the past with you guys, I had some mission I wanted to accomplish. And I failed every time. I was only trying to help."

"Fuhgetaboutit," Flip said. "You didn't fail, Stosh. Life is what it is. You coulda made things a lot worse."

"We lived our lives," Jackie told me. "Everything is going to work out."

Honus Wagner came over to the head of the bed.

"Do you remember what I told you, Stosh?" Honus asked me. "Remember what I said about being a great ballplayer?"

I did. I remembered it like it was yesterday.

"Yeah," I whispered. "I told you that I wasn't any good at baseball. You told me that the secret to being a great ballplayer is to trick yourself into thinking you already are one."

"That's right, Stosh."

"After that," I said, "I convinced myself that I was good, and it made me better."

Honus nodded his head and stepped back so Jackie Robinson could get closer to me.

"Stosh," he said, "do you remember what I taught

you that day at Ebbets Field?"

"Sure," I told him. "Those bigots on the other teams were screaming horrible things at you, and pitchers were knocking you down left and right. I tried to get you to go charge the mound and beat them up, but you told me that you fight back in your own way. Instead of fighting with your fists, you fought back by showing them how good you were. And a lot of those people who hated you came to respect you in the end."

"You got it, Stosh," Jackie said.

I looked over at Roberto Clemente, who was standing quietly in the corner.

"Before I met you, Roberto," I said, "I was really selfish. I didn't care about anybody else. But seeing what you did made me care about other people, and not just about myself. I'll never forget what you told me—If you have a chance to accomplish something that will make things better for people coming behind you and you don't do that, you're wasting your time on this earth."

"That's exactly what I said," Roberto told me.

"Hey, what am I, !@#$% chopped liver?" asked Ted Williams.

Oh yeah. Ted might have hit as many homers as Babe Ruth if he hadn't spent four years in the prime of his career fighting in World War II and the Korean War.

"I tried to talk you out of joining the military," I said. "But you told me that some things are more important than hitting home runs."

"You're !@#$%^ right!" Ted said, which made everyone laugh.

Babe Ruth came over next. He threw an arm around me and put me in a friendly headlock.

"You remember what *I* taught you, don'tcha, kid?" he said. "Swing for the fences. Swing big, with everything you've got. Hit big or miss big. Live as big as you can."

"Yeah," I said. "And Shoeless Joe taught me that sometimes life isn't fair, but we've gotta deal with that. And Satch, you taught me there are no second chances. If you want something, you've got to go get it. Because nine times out of ten, if you let something slip away, it's gone forever."

"I guess if ya go where learnin' is flying round," Satch whispered, "some of it's bound to light on you."

I had remembered just about everything they had told me, and I realized that each of them had given me a little bit of wisdom. When I followed their advice, it made me a better player, and a better person.

"Well, I *know* you didn't learn nothin' from *me*," Flip said, "'cause I don't know nothin'."

"Oh, I learned a *lot* from you, Flip," I told him. "You taught me everything I know about baseball. And something more important, too. You taught me that sometimes you can change history, and sometimes history can change *you*."

We talked late into the night about baseball, life, and so many other things. At some point, I must have dropped off to sleep. When I woke up in the morning, they were all gone.

It was over. But I would have their baseball cards to help me remember them forever. And the rest is history.

Facts and Fictions

EVERYTHING IN THIS BOOK IS TRUE, EXCEPT FOR THE STUFF I made up. It's only fair to tell you which is which.

First, all the time travel stuff is a load of malarkey. No matter how many books you read or movies you watch, nobody has ever figured out how to travel through time, and we probably never will. Joe Stoshack, his mother, and Uncle Wilbur are fictional characters. And if you can't find Flip Valentini's name at the Baseball Hall of Fame, it's because he doesn't exist (although he is named after my good friend Fred Valentini).

Everything else in the book is pretty much true. The Brooklyn Dodgers were on track to cruise to the National League pennant in 1951, but the New York Giants came from thirteen and a half games back in August to tie them on the last day of the season. Then the Giants won the final playoff game in the ninth inning on Bobby Thomson's "Shot Heard Round the World" off Ralph Branca.

If you ask historians what was the most famous home run in baseball history, they will probably name that one. In 1999, the U.S. Postal Service even issued a stamp commemorating the moment. You can watch the homer yourself on YouTube and hear Russ Hodges's famous call: *The Giants win the pennant! The Giants win the pennant!* " Search for "Bobby Thomson."

Over the years, there were rumors that the Giants had cheated by stealing signs with a telescope hidden in the center-field clubhouse. But it wasn't until the 1990s that *New York Times* sports columnist Dave Anderson started talking about it in print. Finally, Joshua Prager blew the lid off the story in a January 31, 2001, article in *The Wall Street Journal.* He turned that article into a 2006 book, *The Echoing Green: The Untold Story of Bobby Thomson, Ralph Branca and the Shot Heard Round the World.* Thanks to Prager's exhaustive research, we now know that the Giants never would have caught the Dodgers if they hadn't been stealing signs. There never would have been a playoff, and Thomson never would have even come to bat, much less hit the historic home run.

To be fair, Bobby Thomson always denied that he knew what pitch was coming. He claimed that he was concentrating so heavily that he never looked over to the bullpen for the sign. He did tell the *New York Times*, "the Shot was the best thing that ever happened to me. I guess people remember me because of that moment. They wouldn't have paid much attention to me if that hadn't happened."

Bobby was traded to the Milwaukee Braves in 1954, and he also played for the Cubs, Red Sox, Orioles, and Giants again before he retired in 1960 with a lifetime average of .270. After baseball, he became a paper products salesman. Bobby Thomson died in 2010 at the age of eighty-six.

Ralph Branca, I think, is the more interesting character. After giving up Thomson's home run, his career nosedived. He hurt his back and retired in 1956. Branca became an insurance salesman, but briefly became famous again in 1961 when he won seventeen straight games on the TV show *Concentration*. He was also the president of BAT (Baseball Assistance Team), an organization that helps needy ex-ballplayers.

In 2011, eighty-five-year-old Catholic Ralph Branca was back in the news when—much to his surprise—he found out that his mother, Kati (and he and his sixteen brothers and sisters), was Jewish, and that several of his relatives were killed in concentration camps during World War II.

After the home run, Bobby and Ralph generally avoided each other. But as they grew older, they took advantage of their moment in history and made a lot of money together signing autographs of photos and memorabilia.

"I lost a game," Branca said, "but I made a friend."

Branca and Thomson

Willie Mays went on to become one of the greatest and most beloved players in baseball history, finishing his career with 660 home runs, two MVP awards, twelve Gold Gloves, and of course, membership in the Baseball Hall of Fame.

But in 1951, when this story takes place, Mays was an insecure rookie. He started the season with just one hit in twenty-five at bats. At that point, he sat next to his locker and broke down in tears, telling Giants manager Leo Durocher that he didn't think he could hit big league pitching.

"I was a scared rookie," Willie wrote in his autobiography, *Say Hey*, "so scared that when Bobby Thomson stepped into the batter's box and belted his historic, pennant-winning home run against the Dodgers at the Polo Grounds, I was crouched in the on-deck circle praying to God: *Please don't let it be me. Don't make me come to bat now, God.*"

"If Bobby made an out, it would be my turn at bat," Willie wrote. "I would have been in a position to become the hero, sure, but the way I was swinging I was more likely to make the last out of the season."

It's doubtful that Willie Mays would have quit baseball if he had hit into a season-ending double play. He was just *too* talented. Admittedly, I invented that possibility for the sake of the story. But Willie also wrote this in his autobiography: "*Who knows, if I had come to bat one more time that year, there might not have been as much history to write about after all.*"

Everybody knows how the regular season ended in 1951, but hardly anybody remembers what happened in the World Series. According to Joshua Prager, the Giants were afraid they would get caught using the telescope and they did *not* cheat in the World Series. Maybe that's why they lost. The Yankees beat them four games to two. The Giants *did* win the Series a few years later in 1954, and didn't win another one until 2010.

Six years after the Shot Heard Round the World,

the Dodgers and Giants both left New York and moved to California. The Polo Grounds, where this historic game was played, was demolished in April 1964. Today, you'd never know a ballpark was there. But if you look around the apartment complex that stands on the site, you'll find a plaque on the wall at the exact location where home plate used to be— the spot where Bobby Thomson hit what came to be called "The Shot Heard Round the World."

Willie Mays—Lifetime Statistics

Year	Team	Games	At bats	Hits	Doubles
1951	Giants	121	464	127	22
1952	Giants	34	127	30	2
1954*	Giants	151	565	195	33
1955	Giants	152	580	185	18
1956	Giants	152	578	171	27
1957†	Giants	152	585	195	26
1958	Giants	152	600	208	33
1959	Giants	151	575	180	43
1960	Giants	153	595	190	29
1961	Giants	154	572	176	32
1962	Giants	162	621	189	36
1963	Giants	157	596	187	32
1964	Giants	157	578	171	21
1965	Giants	157	558	177	21
1966	Giants	152	552	159	29
1967	Giants	141	486	128	22
1968	Giants	148	498	144	20
1969	Giants	117	403	114	17
1970	Giants	139	478	139	15
1971	Giants	136	417	113	24
1972	Giants/ Mets	88	244	61	11
1973	Mets	66	209	44	10
Total		2992	10881	3283	523

Two-time NL Most Valuable Player
NL Rookie of the Year
12-time Gold Glove winner
24-time All-Star
Led the NL in batting, slugging, runs, hits, triples, home runs, walks, and stolen bases
Hall of Fame 1979
Major League Baseball All-Century Team

*Willie missed the 1953 season because he was serving in the military.
†After the 1957 season, the Giants moved from New York to San Francisco.

Triples	Homers	Runs	RBI	Walks	Steals	Avg.
5	20	59	68	56	7	.274
4	4	17	23	16	4	.236
13	41	119	110	66	8	.345
13	51	123	127	79	24	.319
8	36	101	84	68	40	.296
20	35	112	97	76	38	.333
11	29	121	96	78	31	.347
5	34	125	104	65	27	.313
12	29	107	103	61	25	.319
3	40	129	123	81	18	.308
5	49	130	141	78	18	.304
7	38	115	103	66	8	.314
9	47	121	111	82	19	.296
3	52	118	112	76	9	.317
4	37	99	103	70	5	.288
2	22	83	70	51	6	.263
5	23	84	79	67	12	.289
3	13	64	58	49	6	.283
2	28	94	83	79	5	.291
5	18	82	61	112	23	.271
1	8	35	22	60	4	.250
0	6	24	25	27	1	.211
140	660	2062	1903	1463	338	.302

Permissions

The author would like to acknowledge the following for use of photographs and artwork: Robert Edward Auctions LLC (page 12), the National Baseball Hall of Fame Library in Cooperstown NY (22, 25, 42, 44, 58, 64, 75, 77, 89, 151), Nina Wallace (57), and Howard Wolf (153).

About the Author

Willie & Me is Dan Gutman's twelfth Baseball Card Adventure, and the final one in this series, which started back in 1997 with *Honus & Me*. He is also the author of the Genius Files series, the My Weird School series, *The Kid Who Ran for President*, *The Homework Machine*, *The Million Dollar Shot*, and many other books for young readers.

To find out more about Dan and his books, go to www.dangutman.com.

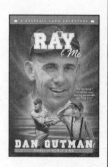

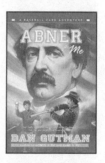

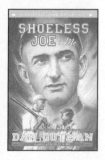